Breaking the Surface

Amanda Zieba

Published by Amanda Zieba
Copyright January 2014

ISBN: 978-1494808464

Type Sets: Bookman Antiqua, MV Boli,
BernardFashion MT, and Agency

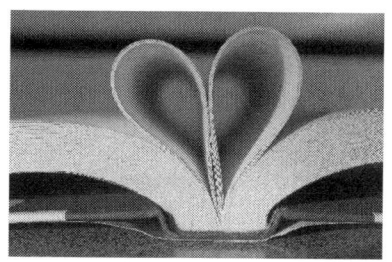

Dedication

To my students, who continually find adventure and wonder in books. It is a joy to watch you fall in love with reading every day. It is my hope that this book teach and entertain you, impress and inspire you, but mostly I hope that it keeps you reading and searching for the next great book.

11 Years Ago

Prologue
Surface

Bay City, Florida – Associated Press

Mayor Robert Christian, university scientists, and worldwide environmental supporters gathered in the Bay City University Library to celebrate the launching of an historic scientific endeavor. The Animal Regeneration Kingdom (also known as the ARK) will be "open for business" later this week when 11 scientists and their families take up residence. These highly specialized individuals will relocate their lives for an undetermined amount of time and dedicate their lives to the cause of science and humanity.

World-renowned professor Solomon Sorenson is putting his master mind, as well as his well-supplied bank account and award winning university science department, behind this groundbreaking project.

"Our goal is to formulate and test a liquid amalgam that will literally eat polluting particles in the water surrounding the coral reef, allowing sea life to regain their hold and flourish in the area. We know it is an ambitious goal, but we've got a great team on board."

Leading the dynamic group is Dr. Arthur Brinestone.

"I've done some pretty interesting things in my scientific career, but nothing like this. This unique experience is the dream of a lifetime for those of us involved in the pollution study. We hope to make a big impact on water pollution reversal for both animals and humans."

The group will be under the constant surveillance of the Surface Station operated by university scientists under Sorenson's watchful eye. The world is waiting in pleasant anticipation for the greatness that is sure to come from this high profile project.

Present Day

Chapter 1
ARK

"The greatest glory of a free-born people, is to transmit that freedom to their children." – Havard

Flynn knew she was awake, but she didn't open her eyes. She was attempting to savor the final moments of her dream. Maybe if she snuggled way down deep into her covers, she could still feel the heat of the sun kissing her pale skin with a million little rays of happiness and warming her near black hair that stretched down to touch her shoulder blades. But no. She wasn't dreaming, she was awake. And she wasn't standing in the sunshine, she was stuck at the bottom of the ocean.

Even as the faint memory of her dream faded, a smile stretched across her lips. She had been waiting for this morning for a very long time. The appeal of spending another second in bed suddenly left her.

SPF 75? Check. Sunglasses? Check. Flip-flops? Check. Lip Gloss? Check. She flung back the covers.

Goodbye goggles. Goodbye wet suits. Goodbye seafood. Goodbye brothers! She slid her perfectly self-pedicured toes into fuzzy pink slippers and plugged her earbuds in place.

Hello sunshine. Hello birds. Hello wind! Hello cheeseburgers. Hello dating! She danced around her room and packed her belongings into a dust covered suitcase.

Eleven years. Eleven years I've waited. It seems as if the years have passed abysmally slow. Like I have been dropped and forgotten at the bottom of a black hole in the ocean. Oh wait, I have. And now? All these years later… Freedom has finally come for me. Freedom at last!

As she danced and packed (a make-up bag just barely

able to zip, her 12 most recent magazines, a Jacque Cousteau biography and her favorite purple glitter nail polish) her smile grew, remembering the day her crazy wonderful journey officially began. It was six months ago.

Flynn's parents, Arthur and Bermuda Brinestone, are scientists. Her parents had been hired by Professor Solomon Sorenson to study the ocean. Well, study the ocean is an understatement (barked Flynn's silent commentary when told the story for the umpteenth time at a dinner table with Tubed-in guests). Yes, to study the ocean was their job, but do it they must from the ocean floor inside a bubbled community called the Animal Regeneration Kingdom. Mr. Sorenson, made wealthy from the shipping industry, built them a home at the bottom of the ocean.

Yes, *the* Solomon Sorenson who patented the unsinkable ship paint that had had quite profound success. "Crashes such as the Titanic no longer haunt you in your sleep. Just paint it on and your worries are gone!" Or so the commercial said. Preposterous really, that a layer of paint could protect your boat, cargo and life all in one, but there it was, copyrighted, backed by the US government and making millions. Ever wonder what that S.S. in front of ship titles meant? Solomon Sorenson, S.S., really, I'm not pulling your leg. Solomon Sorenson. But I digress. Solomon Sorenson built Flynn's parents a home at the bottom of the ocean.

And what a home it is. Labs and observation windows, sea gardens and dining halls, luxurious water beds, jellyfish lit chandeliers and technology that could make Bill Gates jealous. The ARK is quite amazing really. Amazing, in every sense of the word.

Flynn and her family aren't the only ones who live there. They are accompanied by 16 others. The selection process for the inhabitants of the ARK was a long and arduous process, but in the end, six families and one widowed woman were chosen to inhabit the ARK. They were chosen to live, work, study and survive in an enclosed underwater environment. Two of the chosen were Flynn's brothers, which she was also desperately (and silently in the moment, though always not so silently in her waking hours) desiring a vacation from. Now two normal brothers, yes, a vacation from two normal brothers would be nice, but a vacation from one know-it-all science brainiac older brother and a pain-the-butt-thinks-he's-so-special-because-he-was-the-first-person-to-be-born-in-the-ARK-little brother... Flynn was practically (in teenage terms) dying for a vacation from them.

So desperately longing for the social normalness of teenage life, Flynn unknowingly entered dinner when a single conversation changed her life.

"Flynn, darling, we know you are feeling a little, well, confined," her mother begins.

Flynn's internal monologue roared *Duh*. Followed by a not-so-internal eye roll.

Her insolence was arrested mid-roll by a single look from her father, Artie Brinestone, famous scientist extraordinaire.

"I'm listening," said Flynn in her best masked manners voice, to which her brothers Caspian and Noah did a not so covert eye roll, which was in turn caught by Mr. Brinestone, who executed one of his own.

"As I was saying," Mrs. Brinestone cut in, before her family had entirely lost their eyeballs to the backs of their heads, "We have noticed that you have been a bit restless lately and we wanted you to know of a certain opportunity that has arisen."

At these words, Flynn's full attention was focused on her mother and the words coming out of her mouth. Flynn was staring right past the seaweed salad stuck in her mother's teeth and put all her energy into comprehending the message she was about to deliver.

"An opportunity," she continued, "to exchange places

with a student from the surface school for the school year."

With these most recent words, Flynn's jaw flew open as if on hinges. Caspian and Noah also stared, unable to fully believe what their mother was saying. Finally she finished, "We were wondering if you would be at all interested in partici-"

"Interested?!? Interested?!?" Flynn squealed almost hysterically, jumping from her seat. "Interested!?!"

Mr. Brinestone exasperatedly dropped his soup spoon with a loud clank into the bowl, splattering clam chowder across the other members of the table.

Flynn, who would have normally been repulsed by being covered in clam chowder, any kind of chowder really, simply swiped it away from her eyes, pushed her chowder covered hair off her face, got up from the table and kneeled on the floor next to her mother's chair. She stared up at her mother's near mirror image face, her green eyes pooling with tears of extreme emotion.

"Really mom? You are not just toying with my adolescent emotions? You are really thinking of letting me go to the surface school for… for… nine whole months?"

No one at the table breathed until Mr. and Mrs. Brinestone uttered a soft, but resolute, "Yes."

And with Flynn's exhale, came a smile, a smile that had been gone for a long time. But now that it was back… it had enough power to have lit the whole ARK for a week.

This is the smile she had now, as she danced around her room thinking of the adventures she was about to have at the surface school. Free from her calculated way of life, free from constant supervision, free to make her own choices, free from her brothers and free to rediscover a great place that she had dearly missed, a place that she still considered home. A place called land.

There is a reason people used the phase "Homeland". She thought. She tossed a fifth pair of shoes into her bag. *The malls, boys and friends won't be bad either.*

Chapter 2
ARK

"It is interesting to leave a place, interesting to think about it. Leaving reminds us of what we can part with and what we can't, then offers us with something new to look forward to, to dream about." – Richard Ford

After a quickly eaten breakfast, Flynn did one last sweep of her family pod looking for anything she might have forgotten to pack (even though she had double and triple checked the packing list she had been agonizing over for months). She checked mostly so her mom would stop asking her if she had everything, because every item she laid eyes on was needed for survival in the aquatic life, not for her sun filled surface life. She did, however, shove her converter into her pocket at the last minute. (A converter is like a calculator that uses scientific formulas to solve equations for checking water purity.) In the ARK is it necessary to check the salinity of water to make sure it is adequate to drink. It also doubled as a communication device, having a transmitter and communication component embedded. Basically it was a fancy walkie-talkie-calculator-thingy-ma-jig. *It might come in handy with homework or a science fair project. Even if land life does not require constant calculations.*

She gifted rare hugs to her brothers and shoved her expertly packed luggage into the Tube before returning to her mom for one last really good hug.

"Enjoy your time on the surface," Mrs. Brinestone said, fiercely hugging her daughter.

"I promise I will," Flynn whispered back, suddenly emotional.

Flynn pulled away from the embrace and was shocked to see the people of her underwater prison had quietly gathered to wish her farewell. She almost didn't mind that saying goodbye to each of them individually delayed her leaving. Almost.

Finally she stepped into the Tube to join her patiently waiting father. She offered up a small wave and a smile to her departure party. She half laughed, half sobbed when they sent out a chorus of cheers and goodbyes to send her off.

The Tube doors and Flynn's eyes simultaneously closed. *I can't believe this is happening. I can't believe this is actually happening.*

The Tube takes 63 minutes each way, two hours and six minutes round trip. Flynn spent the first 14 minutes sitting with her knees pulled up to her chest and leaning against the Tube wall, mindlessly watching the ocean scenery pass before her. She spent the final 49 minutes pacing restlessly in the 6 foot by 6 foot cube.

Time could not pass any slower. She tugged on her shirt and examined her reflection in the tube glass wall. A reflection of dark hair touching pale shoulders and the occasional glint of a sequin from her flip flops met her stare. *What if I don't fit in? What if Florida public school kids don't follow magazine fashion trends? What if, please Poseidon no, they wore uniforms?* She shrugged, resigned to the fact that she could do nothing about her outfit now, and prayed it would be deemed acceptable. With a last glance at her outfit, she pushed her worries aside and continued her pacing.

The Tube docked in the loading station and then, truly, time passed in slow motion. Artie considered passing on some last minute fatherly advice, but he decided against it. Instead he reminded her that it took another 12 minutes to dock, repressurize, and connect the loading ramp. That thought only frustrated Flynn beyond the point of reasonable sanity and Artie wondered why he bothered to say anything at all. As Flynn took up her pacing again, her father deliberated if he was beginning to see the carpet wear thin in her tracks.

Chapter 3
ARK

"People don't want their lives fixed. Nobody wants their problems solved. Their dramas. Their distractions. Their stories resolved. Their messes cleaned up. Because what would they have left? Just the big scary unknown." – Chuck Palahniuk

The small crowd broke up quickly. Before the wake of the Tube had cleared, many left to begin their day's work. Deep in discussion they filed out the door in pairs or small groups leaving the remaining three members of the Brinestone family standing alone. They stared at the tiny bubbles of water disturbance that were the only lingering signs of Flynn and her father.

"With Flynn on the up and up, literally, you boys will pretty much have the reign of the pod," said Mrs. Brinestone as she stood behind her boys, a hand on each of their shoulders.

"But mom," Noah said exasperated, "why would anyone want to leave the ARK? Seriously! It is beyond cool."

Mrs. Brinestone thought about attempting to explain to her youngest son the dark recesses and complicated workings of a teenage girl's brain, but decided to save her breath. Instead she sighed and said, "Well boys, I'm off to the lab. Try not to worry too much."

She walked out of the room, trying to take her own advice. Caspian hesitantly patted Noah on the back and followed in the direction of his mother without another word.

"Ugh! Doesn't anybody care?!?" Noah shouted after them, and then more to himself, "Flynn would have cared!" Which only reminded him that she was gone and sunk him further into a state of depression.

Not one to sit still for long, Noah gave up his post and began to wander around the home he loved so much. He walked out of the Tube docking station and past the labs where he could see his mother and brother diligently studying polluted water samples among the rows and rows of workroom tables. Today the tables were covered in seaweed soaking in a variety of portable tanks, last week it was octopus tentacles. Who knows what tomorrow would bring? He rolled his eyes and picked up his pace.

Soon he found himself surrounded by computers and digital screens displaying the thousands of factoids needed to keep the ARK in perfect balance. Water temperature, air pressure, oxygen level... the list went on. Even at age 10, and even though he had lived here his entire life, it was all still pretty impressive. He drifted past the classrooms, careful not to attract the attention of Professor Bebee. He wasn't really in the mood to learn, or talk to anyone right now.

His steps took him up the stairs and over a walkway where he stopped to look out at his favorite view. From here he could see both the Observation deck and the Obscoral tank. In front of him stood a 50 foot wall of glass, and beyond the glass... the ocean. *How could anyone want to leave this?* Noah shook his head to clear his thoughts, causing his black hair to swish in front of his familial green eyes.

He directed his attention to the Obscoral tank. The Obscoral tank was quite possibly the best part about living here, at least in Noah's opinion. The salt water tank was installed in the ARK to house a large portion of the coral reef that was damaged in early stages of building. The scientists involved in the project couldn't bear to permanently destroy the piece of living ocean life, so they installed it in their home as art. For a while it sat untouched, but eventually the residents realized it was the perfect place to teach WakeTec riding. The tank offered a controlled environment without the interaction of currents or predators.

A few of the fathers had gotten a bit zealous in their training and began to add obstacles into the tank for their children to swerve around, evade and dodge. Having mastered the obstacles, the dads intensified the course by occasionally throwing exploding pods of ink into the water from the deck above the tank. The final step in the game was added when several fish collection baskets were hung from the grated deck. Riders moved through the course, avoiding the ink pods, attempting to dunk as many balls as possible into the baskets before the given time expired. Scores were kept religiously and record highs were proudly displayed on a nearby board. Currently Noah held the top spot.

Noah could see Luke and Pac suiting up to play and his fingers itched with anticipation. He halfheartedly waved to them, and could already feel his mood lifting.

"Come on Noah, what's your damage? Stop moping around like a jellyfish," Luke shouted across the room.

"She was kind of a drama queen most days anyway," Pac added.

"Poseidon knows we could use a break from her emotional rollercoaster!" Luke said zipping up his wetsuit.

"So are you gonna stay high and dry up there or are you gonna try and stop me from putting my name at the top of this list?" Pac chided as he pointed to the record board.

Luke revved the engine of the WakeTec and shot a spray of water in Noah's direction.

"You're on!" Noah shouted as he raced to the tank and took his defensive position to play.

As Luke engaged Noah in battle, Mrs. Brinestone gave Pac a magnanimous smile and thumbs up from the observation plank above. For a minute she basked in the blissful thought that at this moment all three of her children were content and happy... something that hadn't happened for a very long time.

Chapter 4
Surface

"A happy person is not a person in a certain set of circumstances, but rather a person with a certain set of attitudes." – Hugh Downs

With a hand shading his eyes from the brutal Florida sun, Mr. Brinestone watched his only daughter walk up and out of sight. He tried to tell himself his eyes were moist only from being irritated by the sun, but he couldn't quite convince himself.

As he turned to walk in the opposite direction he was quickly forced to focus on something other than the heavy feeling in his heart. Paying more attention to his thoughts than his path, he tripped over a large navy duffle bag. When he stumbled to regain his balance, someone else became the victim of his clumsy nature.

Nina Nelson adjusted her glasses to rest on her freckled nose and allowed Mr. Brinestone to help her to her feet.

"Hi, ummm, I'm Nina."

"Well hello. Sorry about that tumble there. Hopefully I didn't bruise you up too bad," Mr. Brinestone apologized.

"No worries, I'm fine. All ready to go," Nina continued anxiously. "My parents," she said pointing to the nearby parking lot, "they wanted to stay, but had a meeting and had to leave, but it's all good. I'm ready to go."

They stood on the boardwalk staring at each other. Finally Mr. Brinestone broke the awkward silence.

"Well, I'd better be going. The return trip is disembarking soon, and if I'm not on it, well my wife will have something to say about it." He started to walk back to the Tube. He turned back to give her a friendly wave goodbye when she ran smack into him.

"We've got to stop meeting like this dear," Mr. Brinestone said as he rubbed his lower back where the bag had dug into him.

"Ah, right," Nina agreed. "I'll give you a little more space. It's just that I am so excited about coming down. I have been looking forward to it for months. I guess I am just-"

"Coming down?" Mr. Brinestone interrupted.

"Yes, to the ARK," Nina continued "I am the other participant in the exchange program. I am Nina Nelson."

"Nina... Nelson," Mr. Brinestone said as if saying her name aloud would jog his memory. "Nina Nelson!" he shouted startling her. "Yes! I remember now. So sorry dear. Yes, you are coming back with me. Down with me! I guess I was so preoccupied with getting Flynn off on her way that I completely forgot," he rambled. "Forgive me."

"Yeah, of course," Nina said with a nod. And when they continued to stand still she asked, "So, ah, which way to the loading dock?"

"Right! This way," Mr. Brinestone said grabbing her duffle bag and assuredly stepping forward. He continued to chat away as he and Nina loaded the Tube.

Wide eyed, Nina buckled herself into the seat that Flynn had given up for pacing, and let out a deep breath. Suddenly Mr. Brinestone looked at her very closely. He noticed the sparkle in her eye and the nervous fidgeting of her hands. Mr. Brinestone realized this was an important moment for her, and he knew he should not ruin it for her by talking incessantly. Instead, he closed his half open mouth, leaned back in his seat, and enjoyed the ride in the Tube, remembering what it was like the first time he rode down to the ARK.

They passed the first twenty-four minutes of the ride that way. Silently. Silently drinking in the sea and its landscape. Its animals and plants. Its mystery and wonder.

It stayed light longer than Nina expected and it was

easy to see the creatures that floated by. Angel fish, sting ray, anemones and a hundred more she had yet learned to identify. As they got closer to their destination, it did get darker, but not the pitch black she had envisioned. Vegetation began to creep into their view, the stalks of seaweed and luminescent sea pens growing up to take advantage of what sunlight was filtering down. Only once did she draw in a sharp breath of surprise as a small lantern shark swam past their window. It was then that Mr. Brinestone confidently reminded her of the fiberglass walls' unbreakable strength. Inch by inch, foot by foot, they sunk into the ocean, a wave of comfort washed over both of them.

Secretly Nina kept a well-worn minutely folded brochure about the ARK in her pocket. She had carried it with her ever since finding out about her acceptance to the exchange program, studying the faces and names of the scientists and their families in the ARK. People were not really Nina's thing. Books were Nina's thing. Books were what had gotten her to this tremendous opportunity, but she did not want her lack of people skills to stand in her way. How embarrassing would it be, to be standing face to face with some uber famous scientist and you can't even remember his or her name, let alone answer his or her question? No. That would not happen to her. That was one thing she could guarantee. She dug into her pocket and felt the brochure, and her thoughts drifted to the picture she liked the most. After dazing into space for a few moments, she drew herself back to reality and attempted to make conversation with Mr. Brinestone.

"How long is the trip, Dr. Brinestone?" Nina asked.

"Dr.?" Mr. Brinestone chuckled. "Honestly, no one has called me doctor in such a long time, I almost forgot I was one. Please, call me Artie."

"Oh, I don't think I could. I'll stick with Mr. Brinestone," Nina said as a blush crept across her face. "So, ah, how long is the trip down?"

"It takes exactly sixty-three minutes from top to bottom, plus an additional twelve minutes to dock and re-pressurize," he answered.

"I think the whole experience would be worth it, just for this ride. It is absolutely incredible." she said awe stricken, her eyes following a sea turtle that was distantly tailing the Tube on its descent.

"I must say that it is a joy to see someone take such delight in this ride. I suppose we all just get so used to it, that we have lost some of our wonder for the whole experience," commented Mr. Brinestone, and added "No need to be embarrassed," as he saw the small red dots on her checks spread across her face. "I meant it as a compliment."

The rest of the trip passed that way; Nina asking questions, Mr. Brinestone answering them with a new found enthusiasm. *This is going to work out quite well,* he thought. *Quite well indeed.*

Chapter 5
ARK

"You never get a second chance to make a first impression."
– Unknown

When the Tube doors opened, a small crowd cheered "Welcome!" in a manner that would have befitted a surprise party. *Apparently, I was the only one to forget that I would have a return passenger,* thought Mr. Brinestone as he looked toward his wife with a smile. *Bermuda, she doesn't skip a beat.*

A small banner was strung across an arching doorway to the ARK and read Welcome! Those who were permanent residents of the ARK or frequent visitors knew that the banner was one that was used for all guests to the ARK, but for Nina, the sight of it brought a wide smile to her face.

Less than fifteen seconds here, and I already feel more at home than I have in the last seventeen years of my life. With that thought, she quickly looked down and scuffed her tennis shoe on the metal grated floor. Looking up, she knew a telltale blush would be on her face.

Nina shuffled out of the entrance of the Tube, prodded forward by Mr. Brinestone. With his hand on her shoulder he guided her towards his family and introduced her to each one, who of course she already recognized, although their appearance had changed slightly since the brochure pictures had been taken. Mrs. Brinestone, who insisted Nina call her Bermuda; Caspian, whose handshake and bold stare with eyes as deep and as green as the ocean issued another deep crimson blush across her face; and last but not least, Noah.

Noah resentfully shook her hand and unlike his brother, refused to make eye contact. In his eyes, Nina was a traitor. She was taking the place of Flynn. That's how he saw it. And he wasn't going to let that happen. However, he quickly abandoned that theory when Nina began to tell him that she was named after an old famous ship. Noah, being named after a famous ship builder himself, dropped all signs of harbored ill will and fell into step with Nina as they walked out of the Tube loading station. As they headed toward the inside of the ARK, Nina turned over her right shoulder looking back to Mr. Brinestone for direction. He nodded and waved them on in, and then turned to talk to his wife about their daughter's land birth.

Noah walked Nina around the periphery of the ARK, which consisted of a metal grated walkway with a railing on one side. On the other side of the waist high railing was a giant fiberglass wall, showcasing the beauty of the ocean. Nina would later come to find out that the wall was made of special-treated, double layered fiber glass, just like the walls of the Tube. No matter the makings of the wall, it gave her the feeling of being in a reverse fish tank, with her on the inside and the fish on the outside. It was a feeling that would definitely take some getting used to. To the right of the walkway were the innards of the ARK, which for the time being would remain a mystery to her.

By the time they made their way around the entire walkway, lunch was ready and being served. Normally buffet style was the method of serving, but for today, and for meals when guests were aboard, the members of the ARK ate family style, with bowls and serving trays being passed up and down one large rectangular table. Think of it as a Thanksgiving feast, with seafood instead of turkey. Today a cold crab salad was being handed around. Living in a place surrounded by water treated residents to a constant supply of fresh seafood. A bonus, if you like that kind of thing… which, luckily for Nina, she did.

As they walked into the dining room, Noah and Nina were deep in conversation. Having moved on from the famous boats and boat builders for which they were named, Nina was exhausting Noah with her hundreds of questions about life in the ARK. She was more comfortable asking this 10 year old her novice ARK-life questions than adults. She was silently thankful that Noah had been her first guide through the ARK. It was not until they sat down for the meal that Nina realized she had no idea where she had left her luggage.

"Umm, Mr. Brinestone, I think I left my luggage in the Tube. Could you, ah, give me directions back... well... back to where ever the Tube is, so I can get it?" Nina stammered and started to stand up. At this point she was embarrassed for having disrupted the meal, and began talking faster. "I mean I don't have to take it to my room right now, but I just, um, well... I left it," and as she finished her face again took what would become her trademark blushed color.

"Sit down dear. Don't worry," said Mrs. Brinestone in between bites of salad, "I asked Caspian to take it to Flynn's room. That's where you'll be staying."

Caspian nodded to show that he had complied. Noah however, whined, "But mom! I thought that since Flynn left, I got to stay in her room!" His face was set in ten year old indignation.

"I'm sorry sweetheart, I forgot that there are other guests being tubed down this week, and the guest pods will all be full. Nina is a part of our family for now, and I think it best that she stay in our family pod. How would you feel, all the way out there on the outer edge guest pods if it were your first night in the ARK?" Mrs. Brinestone asked.

And just like that Noah was back to where he started in regard to his feelings toward the new girl. That's what he decided he would call her. She wouldn't even get a name, "the new girl" is what he would call her.

Mr. Brinestone took this moment of silence from his youngest son to ask his eldest son if he would give Nina a tour of the ARK after dinner tonught.

"Certainly," Caspian replied, nodding again toward Nina. Again, Nina felt the blood rise to her face and silently scolded herself for having so little control over the visibility of her emotions.

"What!" cried Noah, "He gets out of dinner dishes? Man, I get the flush every time. Why did you guys even have a third kid?"

"And we all thought the drama queen had left the building," interjected Pac from down the table.

Everyone laughed, including Noah.

Chapter 6
Surface

"Each friend represents a world in us, a world not born until they arrive, and it is only by this meeting that a new world is born."
– Anais Nin

Thud. Flynn's bag landed audibly on the floor of the second story bedroom in the Nelson home. She couldn't believe that she had already been living on the surface for a whole six hours. Six hours. Six hours of complete and total joy.

Well, not total joy. It was harder than she'd like to admit to say goodbye to her dad at the unloading station. She had swallowed down an incredibly large lump in her throat and tried to look past her father's misting eyes when he'd hugged her goodbye. But after he started to lecture her on the proper use of sun screen and the importance of maintaining an acceptable GPA, she had less trouble waving to him as she walked quickly up the boardwalk toward her new life.

Now she had once again taken up her pacing. This time it was across the beige carpeted floor of the bedroom she would be staying in. She was surveying the room, internally cataloging its contents. A map of the sea floor, with push pins and post-it notes stuck to random places; a stack of National Geographic Magazines with several dog-eared pages making them lose their once smooth and flat appearance; a bed plain, yet decidedly comfy; and bookshelves crammed with volume after volume of encyclopedia, research manual and seemingly important documents.

The bookshelf was accented by several small glass figurines. Flynn fingered one as she stopped her pacing momentarily. It was a seahorse and reminded her of the mermaid figurine that she had carefully positioned in her own room. It sat so that she could see it when she laid down in her bed and turned her face outward away from the wall.

Her grandmother had given her the statuette the day before they left for the ARK for the very first time. She hugged Flynn tight, with tears in her eyes, and asked her to look for the ladies of the sea while she lived down there. Her grandma had always been one to fall in love with the mystery of the unknown and belief in what seemed at moments impossible. She passed that love and passion on to those close to her. Flynn remembered rainy days at her Gram's house, with candles lit and playing cards strewn across the floor, playing Solitaire for pennies. Despite Flynn's dislike for things from the sea, the glass mermaid kept a place close to her heart, because her grandma had died a few years after they had moved to the ARK. It was one of the few strong memories Flynn had left from her life on land. She later named the mermaid Marilyn, after her grandmother. In this moment she regretted not bringing it with her to land.

A knock on the door made Flynn abandon her thoughts and her pacing. She walked to the door and opened it to find a girl in trendy sweats, the kind not made for sweating in. Her strawberry golden hair was pulled off her flawlessly made-up face in a ponytail to expertly exude careless beauty.

Nora.

Nora walked in and sat down on the bed previously belonging to her sister. She crossed her legs and sat looking at Flynn. Flynn sat down on the floor, knees tucked up against her, and looked back. An unannounced staring contest ensued until finally, they both started to giggle. And once they started, it became impossible to stop. Mrs. Nelson, upon hearing it, and continuing to hear it, walked upstairs and stuck her head in the door. The girls looked at her, continued to laugh and finally being unable to say anything coherent, waved her off. Mrs. Nelson shook her head and left smiling, wondering what she had gotten herself into. *One Nora is enough to handle, I am not sure what I will do if I have two,* she thought as she walked back down the stairs.

Finally, the necessity for air won over, and their silliness subsided. They lay back breathing hard. Nora spoke up first.

"I knew from the moment I saw you, you were not what I had been having nightmares about for the past six months," said Nora.

"Nightmares?" questioned Flynn, leaning up on one elbow and flipping her legs to one side so she could lay out.

"Yes! Nightmares!" exclaimed Nora. "What would you think if you heard a girl from the bottom of the ocean was coming to live with you? A girl who had been cut off from the normal world for like, ten years!"

"Eleven years, and don't worry, I have been dying to come back to land for about nine of them."

"Well, my sister- she went down in your place- had lived on land her whole life, and she's well... well... just look at this room! Do I need to say anymore?" she laughed.

"Don't worry Nora. I have spent years trying to become a normal surface teen," Flynn said sounding a bit wounded.

"Hey, hey, I'm sorry. That came out wrong" Nora started. "All I meant to say was I can tell you aren't like my sister. I mean, I can tell already that we have a lot in common. Great taste for starters. I absolutely love your shoes. Where did you get them?"

"Ah, thanks, um, these came from a catalog. Actually all my clothes do," Flynn began to explain.

"Really?" asked Nora with her eyebrows arching. She heaved Flynn's suitcase off the bed and onto the floor.

"Yep. No shopping malls under the sea," Flynn groaned crawling up to the bed to mirror Nora's cross legged position.

"Wow, yeah, bummer."

"Well, I guess it's not all awful. I mean my mom and I send for catalogs from all over the place. These shoes are from Japan. We just fill out the forms, and Tube them up. Wait like a million months, and then, they Tube 'em back down. Shoes never get dirty... I never go outside... so I guess I have a pretty extensive collection. Not much else to spend your allowance on down there," Flynn explained as she got up and began to unload a stack of clothes and slide them into a drawer.

"What do you mean, Tube them up?" Nora asked carefully, wanting to get the underwater lingo correct and also not offend her hopefully soon to be friend.

"Well, we have this thing called the Tube. It is like a giant glass elevator that takes things and people up and down. It only goes when there are scheduled trips, so sometimes you have to wait awhile for things to go up or come down," answered Flynn, who continued to unpack.

"I see."

"So, I suppose you were right in worrying. We are pretty cut off from the rest of the world down there," she stopped moving around the room, finding a new home for her belongings. "But don't worry, for real, I watch TV. I even have Facebook and everything! I subscribe to US Weekly... I know everything about surface celebrities. They might as well be my best friends, because I know more about them than anyone else besides everyone in the ARK."

"The ARK?" questioned Nora again.

"There will be plenty of time to tell you all about it Nora, but could I ask you a favor?" She almost dared not to ask it. Almost hoped against hope that this girl would be the friend she had been looking for, for... well, for like, ever. "It's Thursday right?"

"Yeah, so?" asked Nora

"And, it's almost 8:00 right?"

"Uh-huh," replied Nora. And suddenly she knew what Flynn was asking. A smile spread across both of their faces.

"LA Living!" they cried simultaneously and rushed downstairs to lose themselves for an hour of TV drama.

Chapter 7
ARK

"Maybe I was naïve, got lost in your eyes, I never had a fighting chance." – Taylor Swift

Surprisingly, a morning without Flynn started just like a morning with Flynn. Waking up, breakfast in the dining pod, and off to classes. Noah thought something would feel different, but aside from a lack of congestion in the bathroom, everything was the same.

For Nina however, nothing was the same. It was all new. It was all blessedly, wonderfully new. Breakfast was some sort of sea creature eggs with toast, which would take some getting used to, but who couldn't use a change from the mountains of generic cereal they had stocked in her house at home?

After breakfast, the children went to classes. Nina had been instructed by Mr. Brinestone to shadow his sons' movements throughout the ARK. When the boys' activities differed, she was to follow Noah.

Nina thought back to the tour Caspian had given her of the ARK last night after the day's orientation activities. No brochure or website could possibly do the ARK justice. How could you possibly describe a jellyfish chandelier? An underwater farm? Rows of Waketecs? (Underwater jet skis, for you surface folk). A three story window with surrounding observation deck? How do you put into words or snapshot pictures these incredible views? Nina was sure now, after she'd seen it in real life, that it was an impossible task to tackle.

Leaving their family pod (and a grumbling dinner dish washing Noah) behind sliding doors, an awkward silence had haunted the pair until Caspian robotically began his tour. She could tell that he was nervous, and she was too... although she wasn't sure if they were nervous for the same reasons. More than once she reached into her pocket for a phone that she no longer had, to text a friend about her handsome escort. The impulsive attraction was so unfamiliar she had a hard time managing paying attention to Caspian's clearly practiced speech.

"The ARK, stands for Academic Regeneration Kingdom," he began.

"I know, I read the pamphlets." Nina absent-mindedly interjected and immediately was embarrassed she had interrupted. "Sorry." she said, trying to fight her immediate reaction of blushing.

"No, feel free to voice your thoughts."

Nina hesitated while weighing the honesty of his words. She calculated that his expression matched his opinion, so she continued in rare confidence.

"Alright then, to be honest, I have more than a clue."

Caspian raised an eyebrow and it made Nina regret her choice to speak her mind. But then, something quite remarkable happened.

"Don't be so sure," Caspian said with an equally rare mischievous grin. "And don't worry about Noah. He's just upset because Flynn left. We've never been apart before. Our family I mean. It's just something he, I mean we, have to get used to."

"I understand. He's young," Nina said nodding, her bangs shielding her face from his view.

"It's more than that." Caspian paused and tried to come up with words that could fully explain what he was thinking. "When your whole world has consisted of only 21 people, in your entire life, things run deeper than they seem. There's more to Noah than your average ten year old boy."

After that brief lapse in Caspian's seriousness shell, the

rest of the tour continued with programmed speech, Caspian leading, Nina following. Nina asking questions, Caspian answering. Nina's curiosity of the sea and the workings of the ARK far outshone anything Caspian expected. But he enjoyed showing her around, answering her questions, and pointing out little things he had learned in his lifetime of living in the ARK. They passed hours away that first night, wandering and walking and talking. Asking and answering. Teaching and learning. Caspian enjoyed leading Nina, showing her every inch of the ARK, seeing his world fresh through her eyes; especially when those eyes were the bluest he had ever seen.

As he lay in bed that night he had the tiniest moment of gratitude for Flynn. Before falling asleep, he thought, *I might just have to thank Flynn for heading to the surface and sending such an interesting person back as her replacement. Thanking my sister for yet another one of her selfish acts? Now there's a new concept.*

Chapter 8
Surface

"A dream is a wish your heart makes, when you're fast asleep."
– Cinderella

Please let last night be real. Please let last night be real, Flynn thought as she lay motionless in bed. *Please let me open my eyes and be in the Nelson house. Please, for the love of Poseidon, please.*

She didn't open her eyes. Not quite yet. She thought through the events of last night. Nora sitting on the couch opposite her, sipping soda and munching popcorn, watching the most current episode of their favorite reality show *LA Living*. Nora was incredibly patient and enthusiastic as she answered Flynn's endless supply of questions about the characters and how they ended up to be where they were. (Since Flynn had relied on watching the seasons once they had been released on DVD editions, she was a bit behind on the current scenes and events. Nora promised they would rent the last season on DVD from something called Netflix, so Flynn could get caught up for real.)

After the show, the girls talked long into the night. They talked of the surface school, which Flynn learned was called Bay City Public High School. Flynn learned about the classes, teachers and most importantly to her, the everyday drama of Nora's social world: a world that Flynn desperately longed to be a part of.

Because Flynn and Nora were both socially conscious individuals, they stayed up late into the night developing a plan for Flynn's arrival on the surface school scene and also for her public launch into popularity. They came up with many scenarios before they decided on the final plan of action.

First they thought about lying and saying that Flynn was a foreign exchange student from another country. But when the details of home country knowledge and an accent became tricky, they abandoned that plan. They thought about telling people she had just moved to town. But a 15 year old girl without a family all on her own also wound up sounding a bit suspicious. Stories of boarding schools, family in the witness protection program and royalty also fell short.

Finally they decided to stick to the truth... or, as they put it, a glamorized truth. The plan had to be fool-proof because it would be tested and scrutinized, surveyed and examined, dissected and analyzed. In her sheltered bubble upbringing, Flynn had been spared the tragedies of mean girl ways. Nora knew Flynn wouldn't be able to avoid them forever, but she hoped that a smooth debut could hold those misfortunes at bay a little longer.

Nora, with nightmares in tow, had not told anyone of "the girl coming to live with them." This way it would be easy to socially ignore her when she attended school and made an earthly fool of herself. Nora was not willing to self-sacrifice her image for the sake of being nice. Mean though she knew it to be, high school was all about self-preservation.

When Nora entered Bay City High School on Friday morning she quickly found her group of friends in a locker cove and began telling them about the delicious surprise she came home to yesterday afternoon: an exchange student, from an underwater city. Seriously, she was telling the truth and if they didn't believe her, then they would when the surprise walked in on Monday morning wearing fabulous shoes. Her name was Flynn, and Nora thought she was one of the most interesting people she had ever met. These are the lines she fed her friends and they ate up every syllable.

Flynn made Nora promise to down-play the scientist family part of the story, because of the whole social stigma that goes along with it. Nora agreed, especially because she didn't know a whole lot about it, and didn't like talking about topics she didn't know a lot about.

Today was Friday, a day for "surface life adjusting," mandated by ARK regulations. Then came the weekend and finally, Monday. Flynn's official entrance into the world of a normal functioning social life with nonscientific teens would have to wait until Monday.

She stretched, yawned, and swiveled her legs out on to the floor. *Ahh, carpet. What a wonderful luxury,* Flynn thought. She walked downstairs to find a breakfast of cereal that had been set out on the counter for her with a note that simply said, "Sorry it's nothing fancy, Enjoy!"

Afterward, she went to her room and dressed in running shorts and a long sleeve shirt. Skipping quickly down the steps, she bent to put on tennis shoes and grabbed the door handle to leave the house.

"Going for a walk?" asked Mrs. Nelson

Flynn jumped. "Oh my gosh!" she said, her hand flying to her chest in shock. "I didn't know anyone was home."

"Well, I couldn't leave you here to *adjust to surface life* all on your own now could I?" she asked.

"You've been reading the ARK pamphlets, haven't you?" Flynn joked and then smiled. "Well, ah, thanks. I'm adjusting just fine I think. I mean, I feel fine. Just fine." Then she remembered to politely add, "Thanks Mrs. Nelson."

"Would you like to take Luke with you?" Mrs. Nelson asked

"Luke? He's here? I thought I was the only one coming up!! If that creep-show has already been around here bugging you, just let me know Mrs. Nelson, I can easily send him back to where he came from," said Flynn with a hand on her hip looking sternly at a confused Mrs. Nelson.

"Um, I'm not sure if we are talking about the same person, I mean thing. Luke is our dog," Mrs. Nelson explained as she pointed through the kitchen to the back yard.

Flynn laughed, "Oh! Yeah! I'm so sorry. I would love to." *Our Luke has many dog like traits too, so this shouldn't be anything I can't handle. Slobbery, flea ridden, smarter than they look...* She was mentally listing as Mrs. Nelson went to the back yard to put Luke on a leash.

A few minutes later Flynn and Luke (the dog) were jogging in the late morning sun; the time of day when the temperature is just starting to rise. At first they just went up and down the street and around the block of the Nelson's home. She didn't want to get lost on the first day, but she figured Luke would know the way back. She trusted that he would. Having faith in an animal's innate sense of direction and territory, she turned off Lakeshore Drive and out into a world she was longing to rediscover.

Chapter 9
Surface

"It is our choices, Harry, that show what we truly are, far more than our abilities." – J.K. Rowling (Harry Potter and the Chamber of Secrets)

"Ah Professor?" Simon called out as he struggled to pack his backpack and stumble out of the aisle of his second row lecture seat. "Professor!" Almost tripping over his shoelace once, Simon pushed out the door and into the bustling hallway, crowded with students and faculty. He called again, "Professor!" and two others turned to look, but not the one Simon needed.

In a last ditch effort, he lunged forward, reached out and grasped a handful of the tan tweed coat he had been tailing. "Professor Sorenson!"

Slowly, deliberately, the large back turned around to face the doubled over and panting Simon.

"May I help you?" the professor asked, clearly annoyed to be touched.

"Ah, yes," Simon started, but the rest of his intended message was lost.

"I'll tell you what son, if it's a concern with the class you have, talk to the TA," said Professor Sorenson patronizingly.

"No, it's not that, well it is, but there's more... I just... need a few minutes of your time," he spit out between breaths.

Professor Sorenson glanced to his right, toward his brainy looking teacher's assistant, looking for a way out of this awkward encounter. Sadly, the TA was paying particularly close attention to his sleeve cuff.

"Professor Sorenson, please," begged Simon.

"Fine, yes, well, if it's important, then stop by during my office hours. They are listed in the syllabus." And he quickly turned away.

"Thank you!" Simon called after him. He instantly dug into his backpack to find his syllabus, and in the process spilled half the contents of his bag on the floor. Students continued to shuffle by, the tide adjusting its flow around him. Oblivious to it all, Simon smiled and stuffed the items back in his bag, happy that his mission thus far was a success.

Professor Sorenson continued on his way down the hallway whispering something unflattering about Simon to the TA.

Chapter 10
ARK

"Education is not the filling of a bail, but the lighting of a fire."
– William Butler Yeats

"You picked a good day to join us, Miss Nelson," Professor Bebee chimed as she and Caspian, along with six other students, entered the classroom. She had been working hard to memorize their names. Obviously there was Caspian and Noah, and then two boys that she couldn't tell apart quite yet (the length of their hair had changed since the brochure pictures were taken, and they just acted so much alike, that it was hard to tell who was who), but their names were Luke and Pac. The last four were: Anton, Carl, Sonora and Stillman. As far as she could tell, Sonora and Stillman were siblings, and everyone else seemed to be only children.

"Really professor? Why is today such a good day?" asked Sonora, a girl with chin length hair. Nina noticed that she was the only other girl besides herself in the class.

"You mean you haven't heard?" Professor Bebee goaded them. Quickly now they all took their seats, mouths closed and eyes wide waiting for the news she was about to tell. They were eager because in the ARK people did not joke around with big news. It was too devastating to bear, when it turned out there was nothing to hear. As interested as these scientists were in their work, they, and their children especially, searched for something meaningful to break up the monotony of each day.

"They have finished the prototype of the pollution eating solution," she said clearly without hesitation or suspense, but she may as well have, because the reaction of the class was as if she had. Gasps echoed off the steel walls.

"Professor! When?" Caspian uncharacteristically blurted, on the edge of his seat.

"Just this morning before breakfast. That is why I was surprised when you all came in, without the buzz of excitement."

Nina wanted badly to ask what the pollution eating solution was and what it exactly would do. But she also wanted to avoid looking foolish. Thankfully, Professor Bebee came to her rescue. With a flourish of her magenta shoulder shawl she said, "Now, let us, for our own sake review just precisely what the pollution eating solution is, and for our new friend Nina, teach her the wonders of science we work upon each day down here at the bottom of the ocean." Nina smiled her thanks, and got ready to take notes.

"Ugh! Thanks for the mindless review, new girl." said Noah

"Stillman," Professor Bebee continued ignoring Noah's immature comment, "Why don't you begin," the professor said.

"The pollution eating solution, also called PE 328, initially started as a suggestion from the United States Congress. They asked if we could produce a product that, when released in the ocean, would react in a positive manner by finding polluted particles in the water and destroying them by breaking them down, basically disintegrating them."

"Thank you, and Anton, please continue," Professor Bebee directed as she walked around the room.

"The scientists of the ARK first looked at nature-made decomposers and dissected them to see what chemical reactions took place between their bodies and the elements they digest. They found those chemicals, extracted them, and the cloned them to mass produce them."

"Excellent, Luke, finish up for us."

"Well, the decomposing chemicals were not enough, so the scientists infused each molecule with a tiny piece of nuclear reacting agent and also an additional protein component, to totally reinforce its power to break things down. Like giving it turbo power. Like earth's super hero against pollution! They produced it in the most concentrated form possible and have it stored and ready to release when, ah well, I am not sure when they are going to release it, but they finished it today!"

"Very good. Very good!" praised the professor. "I just want to add that we call this miracle of science PE-328, because it took us 328 attempts at combining these materials to come up with this exact and most efficient working configuration. Now, Nina, challenge us with your questions."

And the lecture continued. Nina asked, and the other students answered. Professor Bebee commented from time to time, but mostly the students of the ARK supplied the information. Nina was astounded at the knowledge each of them contained and the ownership and pride they took in knowing it. She only hoped that she could learn to emulate them. The passion for learning she already had, but the raw amount of the information their brains held, that, that is what she would aspire to achieve.

**Chapter 11
Surface**

"Times Square can't shine as bright as you." – Plain White T's

Flynn's entrance, or launch as she and Nora jokingly called it, went amazingly well, despite a small, but quickly dispelled juvenile delinquent transfer rumor. Flynn was dressed in a Nora approved outfit and currently walking down a hallway surrounded by a few of Nora's friends. Friends, who Flynn desperately hoped would become her friends one day too. Nora, the social chair on the sophomore student council, had a meeting during study hall today, so she had left Flynn with what she assured her were the most trustworthy of friends, and promised to meet her for lunch.

In the back of Flynn's mind she had worried, only a little bit, about how tough her classes would be. Science obviously would be no problem, as well as Math. English Literature wouldn't be a problem for Flynn either. Reading was one of the few forms of entertainment within the ARK. By the time she was eleven, Flynn had exhausted the ARK's library and sent away for novels. She read anything from various best-selling authors to the classics. So, really, to be more specific, Flynn was worried about History and the incredible excitement of a class called Driver's Ed.

She had survived her first Driver's Ed class. True, some vocabulary and signs were near foreign, but they were reasonably new to everyone else in class too. History however, her next class after lunch, was something that the other students had been studying, and more importantly living, since they were born. Quickly, she put it out of her mind, because lunch time was approaching and Nora was walking toward her smiling ear to ear.

"Has it been a complete nightmare without me?" Nora asked as she fell into step with Flynn and her friends.

"Abysmal darling. Absolutely abysmal," said Flynn dramatically. "No, really it was fine. Study hall gave me a good opportunity to study up on the Driver's Ed handbook. Getting my driver's license before Caspian will make his big brain burst!" Nora just laughed and shook her head as they entered the cafeteria.

Flynn almost stopped dead at the door when the waft of cafeteria food smells met her. *Food, glorious food!* sang Flynn in her head. The prospect of a no seafood diet thrilled her so much, all worries were pushed from her oh so full mind, and she quickly lined up with the other hundreds of kids to get her lunch.

Though it was a difficult choice, she decided on spaghetti, french fries and an ice cream cone. *Not exactly a balanced diet. I'll go for a run after school.* And then she sat for an amazing twenty five minutes and listened to the conversation of six other fifteen year old girls as they talked dramatically about everything and nothing, and most wonderful for Flynn was the fact that the words ocean, scientist, ARK, module, formula and method were nowhere near these young ladies' lips.

The fear of anything social studies in the history persuasion had left her mind. She walked into room 244, chose a seat near the edge of the block of desks facing the chalkboard, halfway between the front and the back. She slipped a fresh notebook and pen out of her messenger bag and settled in for what she assumed would be a brain draining 53 minutes of United States history. Boy was she wrong. Instead, she got the surprise of a lifetime, and a real treat too.

He walked into the room, just as she had finished getting out her class supplies, and miraculously chose the seat in front of hers. She had to remind herself to breathe. And when she did, she inhaled his wonderful scent... a mixture of fresh grass and Armani cologne. She recognized the cologne from a magazine sample she had taped to the back of her bedroom closet door in the ARK. Mr. Dulcarney brought her back to reality and out of her love at first sight and smell haze when he called her name in attendance.

"Brinestone, Flynn?"

"Ah, here." she managed to choke out.

"Welcome," Mr. Dulcarney nodded before moving on to the rest of the alphabet. She learned through the rest of the attendance the boy in front of her was Alex. Alex Christian. In fact, she didn't have to wait long to find out her obsession's name because in this class, Christian comes right after Brinestone.

The rest of class passed with Flynn's head in a dreamy daze. She barely remembered the phrases: "chapter 2," "American Revolution," "Hi my name is Alex," and "class adjourned." She needed Nora, and she needed her now. Unfortunately, she had to get through a 7th hour Algebra class and then navigate the crowded hallways to her locker.

By the time she reached the locker she and Nora shared, the back of Nora's head was bobbing down the hallway, her blonde hair bouncing behind her. Out of breath from the trek through the current of surface adolescents and their oversized backpacks, Flynn opened the door to find a note from Nora on the white board: *Off to soccer practice. See you at 5. <3, Nora.*

Fine. She would just sit it out and wait on the bleachers. The sun was shining, a slight breeze was blowing, and she was happier than ever to be on the surface. *Seriously, who could honestly miss a bubble of steel in a place as amazing as this! I mean I hardly even have time to change my shoes, let alone miss my old life.*

Chapter 12
ARK

"Friendship isn't a big thing. It's a million little things." – unknown

Sure there were lots of science classes. Classes about chemistry and computers. Classes about the ocean floor and plate tectonics. Classes about marine plants and marine animals. Classes about water quality and human impact on the natural environment. But there were other classes too. Math, lots of math. Hard Math that made Nina's brain boil. She was thankful for her last semester's Advanced Calculus class, and good ol' Mr. Olson and the functions of algebraic expressions. Then there was literature class where they covered the basics of the classics, worldly newspapers, and a wide variety of free choice reading that currently included: graphic novels, Hot Rod Magazine, the latest Surface Fantasy series craze, *10,000 Leagues Under the Sea*, *National Geographic Explorers Magazine*, *The Swiss Family Robinson* and a GRE prep booklet. But always, always, there was science.

In the moments between classes and meals and introductory seminars on the plethora of scientific equipment inside the ARK, Nina took refuge in a small corner of the observation deck. There was fake shrubbery there, a potted tree and an oversized arm chair. As much as she was loving her adventure in the ARK, it was nice to have a little haven that felt like home. She spent hours curled up in that chair reading. She would read books, upon books, upon books and take notes, upon notes, upon notes. She tried to take in everything and anything her brain could handle.

It was here that Caspian would see her sitting after dinner. Curious about his own attraction, he walked down one evening and offered to help her with her studying. *For the sake of testing my emotional attraction theory*, he told himself.

And so the post dinner ritual began.

Noah noticed the amount of time that they had been spending together. Whether in an act of jealousy or an attempted revolt against change, he would shoot suction cupped arrows at an invisible target on the observation window. He would shoot just far enough above their heads to leave them free of danger, but close enough to sufficiently annoy. Mr. or Mrs. Brinestone usually pried him away after a few minutes. Although harmless, they knew his anger was misdirected.

Nina was grateful for the fact that she got to see Caspian every day. It wasn't like at the surface school (how funny that she too now called it that!) having one or two classes with the object of your affection, waiting seemingly endless hours for a few glances, the occasional miracle of partner work and the "see ya" on the way out the door to the next class.

No, here it was different. Nina had the opportunity to see Caspian all the time. In fact, Nina was beginning to wonder how difficult it might be if someone down here would want to ignore someone else. With shared meals and scientific progress for the sake of humanity – it's not like you could take a sick day. Not that she wanted to call in sick – or avoid anyone, quite the opposite. She wanted as much time with Caspian as she could possibly manage to get. She just hoped it wasn't too obvious to everyone else.

"So, how are you, ah, adjusting?" Caspian asked one night after dinner as they sat cross legged facing the observation window.

"Pretty good. I mean, it's cold down here. Well, colder that I am used to," Nina said.

"It's the regulated temperature. We keep the ARK at an average of sixty five degrees." Caspian informed, and then thought, *regulated temperature? Average sixty five? Geez brainiac, you couldn't even muster up some sympathy or offer her your sweatshirt?*

"And I guess, well..."

"Yes?" Caspain asked with interest, hoping to cover his could-be-perceived insincerity.

"Can I say something without offending you?" Nina asked.

"Ah, sure," Answered Caspian, his usual air of confidence deflated.

"You all smell like fish!" Nina blurted out. Caspian reacted with a blank stare. "It's just that I'm not used to it. I suppose I will, I mean..."

"Well, ah, I guess that's something that we'll, I mean, I'll have to start working on."

"I'm sorry," Nina said, still giggling.

"You're forgiven," Caspian said, locking his eyes to hers. "Am I?" he tentatively asked.

"Yes, of course."

"Good. Now where did we leave off in Professor Bebee's lecture notes?" he asked sliding over to see what she had written in her notebook.

Together Caspian and Nina would sit and read, and study and look at the ocean, and talk. They would talk about science, talk about their lives before they knew each other, talk about future plans. Where they would go to college, what they wanted to be when they grew up. And so in their time together in the ARK, they grew a deep friendship.

Chapter 13
Surface

"Most of life is about showing up." – Woody Allen

He didn't arrive too early, or too late. He came right smack dab in the middle of Professor Sorensons' office hours. He had checked in with the department secretary, Mrs. Worthington, and was now waiting patiently, in a straight backed chair.

"The worst he can do is say no, right? Right, I mean, I'd be no worse off than I am now. But no- it would be so great... I just have to. Gosh I hope..." Simon muttered to himself while he bounced his knee and chomped his gum. White ear buds hung around his neck, oddly silent for the moment. "Why would he say no? Why would he say yes?"

"Simon?" called the cheery Mrs. Worthington, looking over the rims of her bifocals, smiling at him. "Professor Sorenson will see you now."

Her grandmotherly smile put him somewhat at ease, until he stepped over the threshold of the office door, and stared across the room. Floor to ceiling bookshelves stretched across the expanse of the room, models of the ocean floor covered tables throughout the room, and important looking documents were strewn on every other available space. At the end of it all, in front of a large bay window sat the professor behind a mahogany desk, grumbling to himself.

"Just can't do it. Just can't. We don't have time to waste on such trivial matters. Toilet paper! Comic books! Chewing gum!"

"Ah, Professor?" Simon squeaked. Immediately he cleared his voice as the professor looked up and eyed him suspiciously. "Ah, I don't know if you remember me, I'm in your Oceanography lecture, the one for freshmen." Simon continued when the professor stared back at him blankly, "Right, we ah, talked in the hallway yesterday. You said to come see you during your office hours if I had, ah, a concern..."

Recognition spread across the professor's face, and instantly it soured. "Yes, I remember," he answered.

"Right, well ah, I am here to talk to you about the Surface Station and the ARK." Simon began to talk fast, for fear he would be kicked out before he could finish his request. "I, ah, was wondering if you take interns, or volunteers or community help or anything! See, I am way totally interested in that stuff, obsessed almost. Books and lectures don't help me much, no offense... I just need to be there and touch it!" and at saying this he reached out toward a model, and instantly pieces of it flew everywhere, some even as far at the professor's desk across the room. "I'd, ah, just die and go straight to heaven if you let me, I mean, would consider hiring me to work there." He finished, and then decided to add, "Please."

His request was met by pure silence. Simon waited a few moments and then asked... "Well... what do you think?"

Professor Sorenson was calculating his options.

The boy has a look of persistence about him... like he will not go away easily. If I could get him to leave, he might be back, several times. The interaction in the hallway proved that. On the other hand, what could this boy possibly handle at the Surface Station with out completely setting things in shambles? He'd been the office less than 5 minute and already managed to break something.

The professor looked down, head of white hair in his hands, trying to compose in his mind what he would say to this boy, to make him leave and not come back, when he noticed again the piece of paper in his hand, the ARK Tube requests. Things the scientists and their family wanted... the treasures from the surface that were plain and ordinary to most people, but were luxury items for those below. Things that he surely did not have time to run around town for, or to organize. He also did not want to waste the talents of his super scientists at the station on these trivial errands. Suddenly he had an idea. A perfect solution to make everyone happy. He looked up at Simon.

"Sure, why not. I just happen to have a job in mind."

"Seriously?" yelped Simon, throwing his hands in the air, almost knocking into yet another costly looking model.

"Yes, as long as you promise to leave my office right now, and not touch another thing," the professor begrudgingly agreed.

"Okay. Right. Well, ah thanks!" Simon said and turned to leave. "Wait!" he hollered across the room, "What is my job? What do I do? Where do I go? When?"

"Come back tomorrow afternoon and talk to Mrs. Worthington. I will tell her to have the information ready for you, Mr. –"

"Ludkin, Simon Ludkin."

"Right. Come back again tomorrow for the information and to sign up for your Surface Station orientation. Good day, Simon."

Elated, inflated, as if flying like a balloon, Simon floated out of the office, past the ever smiling secretary, down the stairs and across Bay City University Campus, hardly believing his good fortune.

Chapter 14
Surface

"Let me save you the suspense. This girl you met? She's not perfect. And neither are you. The question is, are you perfect for each other?" – Robin Williams (from Good Will Hunting)

After waiting it out on the bleachers, Flynn decided from now on she would pack her running shoes and get her workout out of the way while Nora was at soccer practice. But sitting on the bleachers, which might as well have been made out of cement rather than aluminum for all the comfort they offered, allowed Flynn time to comprise a list of questions that she would ask Nora about Alex. First and foremost being: is he dating anyone?

They walked from the practice fields to the front of the school, where Mr. Nelson would be picking them up on his way home from work. There was no need for clandestine talk once they arrived on the edge of the yellow painted curb because the other members of the varsity squad were juniors and seniors, and therefore drove themselves home instead of lamely waiting for a ride.

The words burst from Flynn's mouth like word vomit; quick and forceful.

"WhatcanyoutellmeaboutAlexChristian?"

"What?" Nora asked.

"What can you tell me about Alex Christian?" Flynn asked in a measured voice looking down at her feet and scuffing a piece of chipped paint off the curb.

"Alex Christian!" Nora laughed. Flynn's hopes and stomach sank. "Alex Christian, the Alex Christian? Well you do set your sights high," she said while smiling, and Flynn hoped that was a good sign. "I knew you had good taste and secretly I wondered if you'd pick him out." Flynn's patience was wearing thin. She had waited since 6th period and it was now almost 5:15. But she would die before letting her guard completely down in front of such a new friend. A good friend, but still new. Nora sensed her urgency. "Alex Christian is a saint. A beautiful, well dressed, smart as sin, saint."

"Yes, all that I gathered in the 53 minutes I sat behind him in history, but does he have a girlfriend?" Flynn questioned.

"Well, yes and no." replied Nora, and then continued. "It's complicated. See, he used to date the ever unpleasant Savannah. They met ages ago through their parents and the beloved Bay City Country Club. The B triple C as we non-members call it. But finally her incessant whining and manipulation was too much for him and he broke it off."

"Whining and manipulation? We are only fifteen Nora. It can't be as dramatic as that, can it?" Flynn rationalized.

"It can when your father is the mayor of a small town, and there are few in the ocean side city who don't scrounge for his respect and table droppings," Nora explained matter of factly.

"Her dad is the mayor?"

"No, his is."

"I see. And Alex... likes the social hierarchy of tide pool feeding time?" Flynn asked.

"Until recently he seemed oblivious to his standing in this tide pool society as you put it. And now that he does see it, I think a bit of teenage rebellion has ensued at the Christian casa. But to answer your question fully, no, at this particular moment in time, Alex Christian does not have a girlfriend."

Flynn let out a sigh of relief.

"Come on, dad's here. Mom'll want to know all about your first day at school. Be prepared to give a detailed report of classes, teachers, lunch food appraisal and an overall opinion of the American public school system in general,"

Nora teased as Mr. Nelson's car came into view.

"Not a problem. I actually had time to compose a pre-dinner speech while you were out there productively kicking a ball back and forth across grass," shot back Flynn miming a determined and swift kick, landing her foot close to Nora's back end.

"You know who else plays the fabulous game of soccer don't you?" Nora asked with a knowing smile, looking over her shoulder as she climbed into the front seat, shoving her backpack and soccer bag in the available foot space. With that final comment, they entered Mr. Nelson's four door Sedan in a fit of giggles that didn't end until the Nelson driveway was in sight.

Chapter 15
Surface

"Deal with yourself as an individual, worthy of respect... and make everyone deal with you the same way." – Nikki Grimes

Simon had been working at the Surface Station for a little over a week now. He wasn't given a job title, but if he was, it would have been close to "Glorified Delivery Boy." But Simon did not care. He took his job seriously.

Sure, he was mostly running errands, but it was the attitude with which he ran them that made him to superior to any title. To put it plainly, Simon loved his job.

Every Tuesday and Thursday when Simon arrived at the Surface Station (no doubt, huffing and puffing and with his iPod blaring) he would find a list of items on a post-it note near his miniscule cubicle that had been set up near the Tube docking station. He would take the list, hop back on his bike and pedal across town retrieving the desired items, and sometimes making a few deliveries.

The items on the list were requests from the scientists down in the ARK, little things that they didn't want to live without. This is where Flynn's supply of shoes and US Weekly magazines came from.

Today's list included: light bulbs, the energy efficient kind (for Artie Brinestone), M&M's (the BIG bag!) (for Nina- being away from something as simple as chocolate was harder than she expected, and the big bag would last her awhile), the latest issue of Hot Rod Magazine (for Carl), a bag of Starbucks coffee (for Bermuda Brinestone), a specific novel (for Sonora), a pair of hard sole Minnetonka Moccasins (for Professor Bebee, and yes she was aware that these needed to be ordered, and yes she was willing to wait), and finally a jar of peanut butter (for Caspian and Noah, a request that they routinely made).

They seemed like simple requests. Again, most people would view Simon's job as mundane, but not Simon. He was glad he could give these people their simple pleasures, glad to do these small favors for people who spent their lives trying to make the earth a better place to live.

So he bought and carefully packaged each item. He included a little note, thanking them for their life's work in the field of science and included a tidbit of information about life on the surface that he thought they might be interested in. For example, he told Sonora that the book she just requested was being made into a movie – coming out in June – and once it came out on DVD, he would send her a copy. He told Carl the most recent winner in the Busch Cup Series. He didn't know what you would tell someone who requested peanut butter, so he just sent the boys a clipped comic from the Sunday paper.

At the end of each note he signed his name in his student scrawl – Simon - hoping that one day he would be able to meet some of the scientists and that they would recognize his name from the notes he had sent them, over the months they spent in the ARK.

Simon also had a delivery to make this particular day, to the Nelson home on Lakeshore Drive.

Nora opened the door to find Simon in the middle of a personal jam session – bobbing his head and lip-synching a song unheard by her. Not phased at all by what most would consider an embarrassing moment, Simon slipped his earbuds out and let him hang around his neck.

"Nora, who's at the door?" Mrs. Nelson called from further inside the house, and then when she got to the door, "Oh, a friend of yours?"

"Ugh- No," Nora said aloud and then silently, *thank God.*

"No. I'm from the Surface Station. I have a delivery for

Miss Flynn Brinestone."

"Oh wonderful," Mrs. Nelson extended her hand to accept the package. "I'll see that she gets it. Umm, if I may, ask a question – I can't believe I never asked it before – when this whole crazy student exchange started."

"Sure, shoot," Said Simon.

"Would it be possible for me to send a care package of sorts to my daughter Nina? She is currently studying – and living – in the ARK. Would that be – I mean, is that possible?" Mrs. Nelson asked, her voice hopeful.

"Absolutely! That's my job! Taking the simple pleasures of life to the scientists trying to save ours."

"Wow dude, you take your job pretty seriously," Nora scoffed.

"Absolutely." Simon agreed with a nod.

"Do you have a minute to wait? Could I get a few things together to send with you now?"

"Sure, No prob."

"Wonderful!" Mrs. Nelson exclaimed clapping her hands together. "Nora, quick, go pack up some of those cookies and grab a pair of Nina's thick socks from her bottom drawer. I'm just going to..." she trailed off as she rounded the corner to prepare the package for her daughter whom she REALLY missed. Parents don't have favorites, but they do appreciate different things from their different children. No one could ask for a better shopping partner that Nora, but on the daily communication skills, her younger daughter was somewhat lacking. In short – Mrs. Nelson was missing her daily dose of mother-daughter talks with Nina.

The package was put together quickly, but with love. Mrs. Nelson set up a schedule with Simon, so that in the future, she could be more prepared, and her care packages could be more thoughtful.

Fifteen minutes after arriving at the Nelson home, Simon was on his bike heading back to the Surface Station, balancing his load precariously, careful not to lose a single item on his return trip. Satisfied with another productive day of work, he shut off the desk light in his cubicle, leaving behind a stack of carefully wrapped packages, with small notes attached to each, ready to send down in the Tube tomorrow.

Chapter 16
Surface

"And if we blossom as high as northwestern trees, I swear I'll still be the same as I was as a seed. And if these branches hold a leaf, they'll be convictions I believe. This is the beginning of something too strong to break now." - The Starting Line

It has been a month since our leading ladies Flynn and Nina have taken up their new residences on the surface and in the ARK. Things are going splendidly for both of them, and they are enjoying themselves immensely. Settling in in their new worlds was an enjoyable and growing experience full of new foods, new friends, and new places.

Flynn was especially enjoying her new world of fashion and freedom. Without the constant supervision of cameras and brothers, she was free to make more decisions for herself, like her hair color for instance. No amount of sunlight could change her dark brown hair to the golden celebrity blonde she had dreamed of, so Nora helped her dye it with a home hair dye kit. Needless to say, the results were dramatically radiant. (Or at least, that is what the box claimed her hair would look like). The real test, according to Flynn, was if it caught Alex Christian's attention, and it had, so she considered it a huge success.

Nina was the same old Nina, as far as she looked. She had just relocated her life 2,000 feet below sea level, that's all. Except for a few things.

It wasn't just Caspian that Nina enjoyed spending time with in the ARK. While girlfriends weren't Nina's strong suit on the surface, she was convinced that was because she had never met anyone like Sonora.

Sonora wasn't deluded like the other girls Nina knew,

with eyes only for celebrity hunks and the perfect shade of nail polish. Sonora and Nina could talk about science and future life plans without the hindering pretense of having to giggle foolishly or twirl their hair.

They talked about everything and anything, except one thing, Nina's feelings for Caspian.

Caspian felt equally trapped. Before Nina, girls had never been on his radar. When the only girls around are your sister and one other girl you grew up with for the past nine years (not even bothering to count the moms and his teacher) - the topic didn't often come to mind.

Caspian had always planned to go to college on the surface, before coming back to the ARK. He assumed that would be his opportunity to meet girls. But now it appeared the plan had changed. Now that he had met Nina, he didn't plan on meeting any other girls.

Both Flynn and Nina learned that all mothers, while having small differences, for the most part are the same. They wanted to know the minute to minute update on everything in their daughters' lives, even when it wasn't cool to ask. Instead of the usual eye roll they would give to their real mothers, they met these inquisitive conversations with smiles and pretended more as if they were talking to friends than to a mom.

The Tube was busy carrying letters and packages back and forth from mother to daughter. Even though they hid their excitement, Flynn and Nina relished their packages in private, looking forward to the small comforts only a mother can give. Family updates, homemade chocolate chip cookies, the latest best-selling novel and knitted socks for those cold metal floors were the things Nina cherished. Flynn, on the other hand, wanted the progress updates on scientific projects underway, an occasional fresh shipment of crab legs, pictures of her left behind sea pets, and though it was difficult to admit she enjoyed hearing about her brothers as well.

So life moved along for each girl, making each happy in their decision to relocate for a while. Life moved, and it was about to move much faster.

Chapter 17
ARK

"Learning is a rebellion. Every bit of new truth discovered is revolutionary to what was believed before." – Margaret Lee Runbeck

As Nina walked into the dining room on the third day of her second month in the ARK, she could tell something was off. It was as if she could see the steam rising off of Caspian; either that or the storm cloud of emotion that was parked over the heads of the rest of the kids while they begrudgingly shoved spoonfuls of seaweed oatmeal in their mouths.

Nina walked through the breakfast buffet line and then took her usual dining place at the Brinestone family table. She felt a bit traitorous sitting down to eat with the adults, but she had learned through past awkward social situations, that doing what you normally do seemed to yield the best results. Or at least the least damaging results.

"Good morning dear," greeted Mrs. Brinestone. "Did you sleep well?"

"Yes, thanks for asking," Nina replied. "Uh... what's..."

"What's with the new seating arrangements?" Mr. Brinestone completed her question.

"Ah, yeah," Nina said, relieved she didn't have to fill in the rest, for fear of sounding rude.

"It seems the *children* are upset, because we will not include them in the release of the PE-328," Mr. Brinestone answered, with emphasis on the word children.

Mrs. Brinestone nodded and added, "Can you blame them Arthur? We treat them as adults 364 days of the year, asking them to live up to our standards and rigorous academic expectations, and then when something as exciting as this comes along, we tell them that they are too young."

"Are you defending their childish display of rebellion Bermuda? Do you believe they should be allowed to accompany us today?" Mr. Brinestone asked incredulously.

"No. No. I am just saying that I understand their frustration. And no to the second question as well. It is much too dangerous for them to come along. I was just saying..."

"Well don't, because it will give Caspian a leg to stand on in his argument. And you know how well he can debate. I don't think I can withstand another brutal bashing of strong vocabulary this early in the morning. So I am content with his cold shouldered breakfast sit in. Thank you very much."

"Is there room in there?" Mrs. Brinestone asked.

"In where?" he responded quizzically.

"In your mouth for your breakfast? It was so full of words just now, that I am not sure," she smirked. "And you wonder where your children get their high aptitude for verbal abilites?"

"Always have to have the last word don't you Bermuda?" Mr. Brinestone sat pouting, stirring his own bowl of oatmeal.

"You know I do dear."

Nina ate quickly and left the dining room when the rest of the students did, anxious to not hold her recant position a minute longer. She fell into step with Noah, who tossed her a look that clearly restated his opinion of her and that it had, if possible, sank even lower. The students stomped wordlessly down the corridor to their classroom and then slouched into their desks.

Professor Bebee, well aware of her students' mood before they even entered the classroom, pasted on a cheery face and pretended to be oblivious to their outpouring emotions.

Chapter 18
Surface

"High school was about hiding all the things that made me different and trying to fit in somewhere. I didn't know who I was."
– America Ferrera

Monday and Science class had come upon her again. It was a time that made Flynn truly anxious. Even though she loved science, and was off the charts smart in it, her new friends had trouble understanding her advanced levels of thinking and her desire to be more than just a pretty face. It was a precarious balance between being true to her own self, and popularity. A balance that was difficult to maintain. Very difficult indeed.

Today's hallway discussion on the way to science from lunch had been shampoo. However inconsequential Flynn really thought shampoo was, she nodded and smiled her way through the four and a half minute travel time from the cafeteria to the science lab. But as they took their seats she made a monumental mistake. Monumental, in the world of pretty haired girls.

"Showers! So incredibly overrated," she exclaimed. As soon as she'd said it, she knew it was mistake. She could read the look in her friends' made up and glittered eyes.

"I'm sorry, did I hear you correctly Fin?" Savannah said, feigning sweetness. "Did I actually here you say, that showers are overrated?" and now raising her voice enough so that the whole class could hear, "You don't shower?"

Now I have done it. Seriously, how difficult is it for you to keep your mouth shut! Flynn reprimanded herself. But thinking quickly on her feet, which were covered in high fashion shoes by the way, she replied in and equally carrying voice, "For every three minutes we spend in the shower, we use as much water as a person in the African Serengeti uses in an entire day. For EVERYTHING. So, really, I'm just doing my part for like, ecology."

"Ummm, uhuh, whatever science girl," giggled Savannah, impeccably dressed as usual. She tossed her shiny, gorgeous, orange-red hair over her shoulder in one swift movement as she turned away from Flynn and began whispering to the people at her lab table.

But Poseidon save her, Nora came to the rescue. "Just because you haven't mastered the art of showering yet Savann-ah doesn't mean the rest of us should be wasteful of our natural resources. And by the way, her name is Flynn, fish face. Nice scales, ever heard of skin moisturizer?"

Simultaneously Flynn and Nora turned to face forward as Mr. Bottleberke began a lecture on Coral Spawning. "Tell me later, how you get everything done in three minutes okay? Shampoo, conditioner, face wash, legs shaved, soap… everything? All in three minutes?" whispered Nora incredulously.

"You forgot brushing your teeth," Flynn said with a smile as she let her mind slip into the science lesson for today while Nora just shook her head in pure unfathomable awe.

Science class ended and the students started to shuffle out of the room.

"Excuse me ladies and gentlemen!" Savannah said in a sing song voice, "I just wanted to let you know that this Saturday night will be my birthday party. The entire sophomore class is invited, because it's rude to exclude people, and I am not rude."

"She must be studying a different SAT vocabulary manual than us," whispered Nora behind her hand to Flynn. This comment caused Flynn to giggle, which caused Savannah to stare, and then continue her verbal invitation.

"There will be music, food and a bonfire. Starts at eight.

See you all there!" she finished, packed up her things and walked out of the room.

"You really want something to laugh at?" asked a girl leaning over to Flynn and Nora's lab table. "That was a rehearsed speech. I heard her in the bathroom practicing this morning before school. She was staring in the mirror practicing different facial expressions."

Laughing and in between breaths Nora asked, "Are-you-serious?"

"For sure. What's not funny is that this is the fourth time I have heard the practice perfected invite. Unfortunately, Savannah and I have a very similar schedule."

"So you're not going?" Flynn asked.

"Of course we're all going," replied Nora seriously. "Unwritten rule of a small town: If there is a party, everyone goes; no matter who is hosting it; no matter who else may be going; no matter how lame it may potentially be. Everyone goes. Because in a small town, you do not pass up an opportunity for something to do."

Flynn nodded taking in what seemed to be (according to Nora and the other girl whose name she did not know) an important lesson.

"So this means Alex will be going?" said Flynn.

"Yes, he will be there," said Nora. "So of course that means that we need to go shopping. And by shopping, of course I mean raiding your closet for some unseen fashion treasure from half way around the world that will make us both look amazing."

Chapter 19
ARK

"The future is no place to place your better days."
– Dave Matthews Band

By lunch the adults had not yet come back from the initial search of the ARK territory after the release of the PE-328. While Caspian found this strange, he did not begin to worry until dinner came and went and still they had not returned. However, he had a little trouble pleading his worried case to the others.

"It's just strange," he said thinking aloud. "Hardly anyone stays out of the ARK after midafternoon unless they are studying the nocturnal habits of organisms. Not that night and day are all that distinguishable at the bottom of the ocean..."

"I agree," chimed in Sonora. "Something is definitely off."

Worries started to ever so slowly seep into their brains. Pac, suddenly put up an instant reservoir against their leaking concerns.

"Are you kidding me? Seriously, are you kidding me?" he said standing up from his eating place.

"A night alone in the ARK, adult free, except for you dear Professor Bebee, no offense intended," and she nodded to show none was taken before he continued. "A night on our own, without the supervision of scientific super power brains to stop us from participating in mildly ridiculous adolescent antics?" Pac looked around the table to see if they were catching his drift and jumping aboard.

"Pac, you know they still have the security and observation cameras on, don't you?" reminded Carl, in a voice not all that different than an adult's.

"Yeah, but they can't do anything right now..." said Luke thinking aloud. "I mean what is the worst they can do to us. Ground us? Please, it's not like we go anywhere. Besides a little mischief and fun is worth a week, or twelve, of kitchen duty. Pac is right. Let's live a little."

And that is how the night of fun began. If only they knew. If only they knew.

The sliding back of chairs was like a gunshot to a race of debauchery. Well, as much debauchery as a group of teenagers can have at the bottom of the ocean. Their form of debauchery included eating an entire gallon of ice cream from the freezer, playing endless rounds of Obscoral and watching surface flicks until their eyes felt like falling out. They even ventured a long distance ARK-to-Flynn call on their converter. But there was no answer.

Nina joined in on the fun, but only half-heartedly. She sensed that something wasn't right. Or maybe she didn't sense it, but just picked up clear signals from Caspian and the way he withdrew from the escapades of the evening. After taking a go at Obscoral and failing miserably, she was pulled out of the tank by Luke with warm words of encouragement telling her that she would get the hang of it in no time.

"You know Luke, on the surface I wasn't too athletic or graceful," Nina said wringing out her hair onto the metal grated deck. "I don't see how millions of gallons of water surrounding me is going to change all that much for the positive. But thanks for the support."

Luke shrugged and left her on the overhead deck as he strapped up and then dove in ready for his shot at Obscoral glory. As Nina stood there toweling off, she saw Caspian sitting on the observation deck, in their usual post dinner meeting spot. His legs were hanging down beneath the railing and he was staring out into the dark water. She wrapped the towel around herself and journeyed across the ARK to sit beside him.

Sitting down, she could tell that he hadn't heard her coming.

"Sorry, I didn't mean to startle you," she started. "I mean, if you want to be alone, I can go."

"No, it's fine," he said quickly. "I mean, please stay," and then they were both silent for a long time.

"You know, my mom calls the observation deck at this time of day SeaTV. It's like our television. You can watch mind numbing, hour after hour, and not even be able to tell anyone what you have seen, but you still do it. I guess it helps me relax."

"I can see that. I mean, why she calls it SeaTV... and why it helps you relax. I like it," she said decidedly.

"They should have been back by now," Caspian said quietly. "I hate to disrupt everyone's parental vacation, but something's not right."

"I know, I can feel it too. But what should we do?" asked Nina.

"I don't know... I don't know."

They sat for a while longer, staring into the dark ocean and the tiny specks of organisms that passed their line of vision. Nina tried once or twice to name a fish she saw swimming by, but eventually she gave up and gave into the mindless staring that seemed to relax Caspian so much. Their SeaTV was only occasionally interrupted by a hoot, holler or cheer from the Obscoral Dome, to which they would both turn over their shoulder and look, before resigning again to their continuous gaze.

But then, not so suddenly, Nina's gaze was not so languid. It began to have a focus. She could not pinpoint the moment she realized something had changed in their marathon episodes, but there was something definitely different about the scene.

"Hey," she said attempting to pull Caspian out of his

stupor, "I think I see…"

"I know." he cut in. "I see it too, but what…" and he trailed off, focusing his eyes on the object coming towards them. It wove back and forth, back and forth. Definitely not human. Definitely not man made either. It came closer and closer.

Because of the darkness at their sea level, it was more of a moving shadow than a specific thing. And the shadow was getting bigger. Caspian and Nina began to stand up, and move away from the sheet of fiberglass wall. Caspian instinctively put his arm across the front of Nina, the way a mom does to her child when she stops quickly at a stoplight. Their eyes got bigger as the object swam closer. It was definitely swimming. That much was obvious now.

The shadow was starting to take color, and then all at once it became clear. It was a blue and green barracuda fish and it swam right up to the edge of the ARK, and then… it spoke.

"Go to the prepatory kitchen. Take your flashlights, sea guide and food. Go now! Do as I say!" The voice was urgent. And for whatever reason, brains numb from SeaTV or pure shock, Caspian and Nina listened.

Instantly they jumped into action. Nina ran to get Sonora from her room where her eyes had been permanently glued to a TV screen of the latest episodes of her favorite prime time show. It took no large amount of convincing with the terrified look on Nina's face and the fact that she added 'Caspian said we have to…' to the message (instead of, "this fish swam up to us and ordered us to…").

Nina and Sonora raced to the kitchen grabbing the dictated items with a few extra essentials and arrived there out of breath. They didn't have to wait long for the boys to arrive in the same state.

"Caspian, what's going on?" demanded Noah. "I was about to break the all time Obscoral record and…"

"Yeah you wish!" shouted Stillman "You just-" but he was cut off.

"You guys!" shouted Caspian desperately. "Please, just listen. Something is wrong. Something is very very wrong." Everyone, now silent, stared at Caspian. "We were sitting on the observation deck, and this fish came swimming up to the glass, and, and..." he didn't know how to proceed from here on out, because he knew that it would be impossible to believe. There was no other way than just to say it. "And the fish told me that we had to come here."

The silence erupted into shouts and laughter and snorts and yells.

"I'm serious!" Caspian shouted. "Ask Nina." And again silence consumed the kitchen and all eyes were on Nina.

Her faced flushed from the attention, she stammered, "I have no idea how it happened, but it's true. We both saw it and heard it."

"Are you pullin' my fins man?" smirked Pac "You couldn't think of anything better to prank us on that this? Psh, you are getting old. You really could use some fresh air you know."

"Pac, I wish I were kidding. But you know my creativity reaches farther than this. If I were kidding, don't you think I would make up something a little more believable, something with proof?" Caspian paused. "Look, I know it sounds crazy, fish talking, whatever. It happened. I don't know why I listened, but I did." After another pause, he continued. "But it makes sense right? If something were to go wrong, where have we always been told to go? In emergency drills in class, where has Professor Bebee always taught us to go? To the inner prepatory kitchen, with food, water bottle and sea guide."

"Where is Professor Bebee?" asked Sonora.

"Oh my gosh!" cried Nina. "I'm so sorry, I completely forgot. Caspian, you said get the girls. I don't think of

Professor Bebee as a girl, I mean she is, but you know, not a girl like us! I'm sorry... I, I'll go get her," Nina rambled quickly.

"No, you are still getting familiar with the ARK. Stillman, Anton, go get Professor Bebee. And keep your eyes out for anything strange," demanded Caspian assuming the leadership position.

Stillman and Anton raced out the inner kitchen doorway and through the dining room. The rest of the kids sat silently in the kitchen, wondering what in the world was going on, and what was going to happen next.

Chapter 20
Surface

"Some things are true whether you believe them or not."
– Nicolas Cage

There she sat, religiously combing her bangs to one side. She always sat this way. Always in science class. Always, especially, when Alex Christian was in the vicinity. Combing, combing, religiously combing her harvest moon colored hair to the right and tucking it behind her ear. Seated on the edge of her stool at her lab table, combing, not using her brain except for an action that by now had become involuntary. *What a waste,* thought Flynn. *What a perfectly good waste of a brain. Poor Savannah Taylor, a waste of a brain.*

But in Savannah's mind, she wasn't a waste of a brain. She was just another (if be it fabulous) teenage girl trying to live her life, exactly the way she wanted it. How was it her fault, or problem, that she usually got her way and what she wanted when she wanted it. In Savannah's mind, there was a girl like her in every town. She was just lucky enough to be "the girl" in this town.

Another science lesson had ensued and Flynn found it hard to concentrate, however interesting Mr. Bottleberke's lesson on wave patterns grew to be. She was unsettled by the call last night from her brother. He had called just as she returned home from the soccer game, still floating on cloud nine after Alex had asked her out. It was Noah. *Probably just a prank right? He has been spending a lot of time with Luke and Pac lately. He is just mad at me for leaving, and this is his way of getting a little revenge.*

This started to make her feel better, and then she replayed the conversation of last night in her mind.

Her converter had been buzzing and vibrating all night long, and finally, as she slipped into bed she answered its call.

"Hello?"

"Flynn- it's me, Noah." (Does he sound out of breath?)

"Noah, hi, did you just come out of the Obscoral Dome? You sound breathless."

"No - listen."

"Really Noah, I don't have time for a play by play of your game tonight. I have to get to bed. I have a really big test tomorrow." (Really she didn't, but Noah wouldn't know that.)

"Flynn!" Noah shouted almost desperately. "Listen, something is wrong. The animals, I, I don't know. Something is wrong. They, they can think! Like people. And talk!"

"Ha ha Noah. Did Luke put you up to this? Or was it Pac, or maybe Professor Bebee? Tell her I am learning a lot up here and won't be behind in my studies at all, so you can all just rest your pretty little heads at the bottom of the ocean down there, because I am breathing free and easy up here."

"Flynn! Seriously, there's-"

And then the transmission cut out.

Nothing can be seriously wrong right? She continued to think, as lab packets for today's experiment were filtered through the class from table to table. *There would have been a news report or something... reporting a change, or a major event in the ARK right? Flynn, get real. Animals? Thinking like humans. Talking? Right, if you fell for that one, they really would think the blonde was getting to you. Snap out of it. Psh, animals with human intelligence. Nice one boys, real nice. But don't worry, I'll get ya back.*

And with that last bit of self-convincing, she opened her lab assignment, pushed her own blonde bangs out of her eyes, chewed on her pencil and dug into her work.

Chapter 21
ARK

"No one is so brave that he is not disturbed by something unexpected." – Julius Caesar

Out of the dining room around the corner and BAM. It was like running into a brick wall. Around the corner of the dining room, was a clear view of the observation deck and staring back at them from the other side of the wall of glass was the largest school of dolphins either Stillman or Anton had ever seen. Even bigger than either of them knew possible to exist. It seemed as if they were all staring right at the two boys. With a look of panic shared between them, they continued on their mission, now with a sense of dread and terror fueling their speed.

Again the looks on their faces and sense of urgency did not leave much room for Professor Bebee to argue about their message to come with them immediately. She hurried faster than most women in their late fifties would have found plausible. When they came through the pod hallway toward the dining room Professor Bebee almost choked with shock as she reeled back at the sight out of the observation deck window. Stillman and Anton ushered her quickly into the dining room and then into the inner kitchen.

It was a moment before they could catch their breath and relay the latest update to the rest of the crew. When they did, it was difficult for them all to not go and take a peek.

"Believe me man, I wish I could give you my look," said Anton

"I know," added Professor Bebee. "I wish I had never seen it. It was such an odd and eerie feeling. It's like being inside the fishbowl."

"Well, that's basically what we are right?" piped up Nina from a back corner. She was sitting on top of a cutting board topped food preparation stand. She knew it was unsanitary, but she didn't think it would be disputed at the moment. "I mean, really, you think you are all down here to look at the creatures and plants. Well it looks like now, they are looking back."

"You should have seen the way they were looking at us. It was like... It was almost like..." Stillman struggled to come up with the words to describe their beady dolphin eyes on him.

"It was like they hated us," said Anton finishing his sentence.

"Yes, yes. It was exactly that kind of look," agreed Professor Bebee.

"But why?" asked Noah, who for the past half hour had said next to nothing besides mumbling under his breath about Obscoral records.

"That, my dear boy, is what we must figure out," said Professor Bebee in her take charge, grown up professor voice. And even Pac would admit, that it was nice to hear the voice of an adult telling them what to do.

Chapter 22
Surface

"I never worry about action, but only inaction."
– Winston Churchill

It was Thursday and another day passed without Flynn hearing from her family. Troubling as it was, it was easy to put out of her mind, because tonight, she had a date. A double date actually. Flynn and Alex were going to the movies with Nora and Riley.

Alex had asked her out two nights before. He stood sweaty, dark hair hanging in his gorgeous eyes, smelling less than sweet. He had just finished a soccer game, a victorious one. The lights from the field illuminated the parking lot, but as he asked her to the movies this Saturday night, tunnel vision allowed Flynn only the sight of his face. When she said yes, he said great, and pecked her on the cheek before running to the locker room.

Flynn tried to remember what they were going to see, but that also had apparently been put out of her mind. Sometimes she wondered if she was getting stupider by spending time on the surface. *You know what they say, you are the company you keep, or at least that is what my mom says. So what does that say about me, hanging out with gorgeous sophomore brains, instead of 20 boring, yet brilliant brains. Pure science would have me losing hundreds of brain cells everyday!*

Her thoughts were interrupted, again, by a knock on her bedroom door.

"Hey, Rapunzel, you ready?" Nora asked peeking her head in through the door.

"Rapunzel, what do you mean?" Flynn, feigning hurt feelings, shot back.

"Would you prefer Goldilocks? Quit fussing with your hair. The boys are on their way. Riley just texted me," Nora instructed.

Together they walked downstairs, ready for a night of laughs, jumbo popcorn, and boyfriends. But something just didn't feel right. That troubled feeling Flynn had so diligently tried to repress kept sneaking up on her. And then Nora nudged her, and she saw the headlights pull into the drive, and they headed out. Four teenage kids just out to have a good time, what could be wrong with that? But still, she couldn't shake the nagging feeling that was still there, in the not so back parts of her mind anymore. It was there, begging to be noticed, begging to be heard. It was there, begging to be dealt with. Sooner or later, it would be all she could think about, like it or not.

The nagging feeling was eating at her all night. Well, if she was honest with herself, she wasn't thinking about it all night. The moment Alex first reached to hold her hand in the theater. His fingertips brought a flash of heat that spread instantly across her hand, up her arm and into her face. She was definitely not thinking about it at that moment. The moment, or moments she felt someone from 3 rows back, (someone being Savannah Taylor) throw popcorn at the back of her head. The moment when the serial killer in the movie jumped out from a closet to grab his next victim. And finally, she was not thinking about her family, as Alex leaned over to kiss her good night before she got out of his car.

It's going to be fine, she thought as she tried to make herself fall asleep. *It's going to be fine.*

Chapter 23
ARK

"People by nature are changeable. It is easy to persuade them about some particular matter, but it is hard to hold them to that persuasion. Hence it is necessary to provide that when they no longer believe, they can be forced to believe."
– Niccolo Machioavelli (The Prince)

With Professor Bebee issuing orders, they came up with a plan in a matter of minutes. Caspian and Noah were to sneak out of the side door of the dining room (there are two entry and exit points in every room, in case of impending disaster and the need to escape). Together they would complete a circuit sweep of the ARK looking for anything out of sorts and any sign of the missing adults. Pac and Luke were to go to the laboratory holding the remaining bottles of the PE-328 and bring it back to the kitchen. The rest of the group would remain in the kitchen focusing on three tasks. Stillman, Sonora and Professor Bebee would compile a list of everything they knew about dolphins, while Nina, Anton and Carl would inventory the supplies they had without leaving the dining room. Everyone doubted the validity of Caspian's story, but Caspian's track record of honesty left them working diligently, despite their denial on the whole talking animal scenario.

At this point, staying inside spaces hidden from those outside the ARK seemed like the best option. So, all movement around the ARK was done stealthily. Having spent the majority of their life in the ARK, Pac, Luke, Noah and Caspian were no strangers to sneaking around without being seen. Pac and Luke accomplished their first mission in record time and were helping Nina, Carl and Anton inventory in a matter of minutes. Caspian and Noah took their time.

Leaving through the side door of the kitchen, they slithered on their bellies to the hallway and then crouched quickly to avoid being seen. From their crouched position they surveyed the scene. What they saw amazed them.

The pod of dolphins was still occupying the view of the observation deck, but as shocking as that was, something else stuck out even more. The dolphins were turned toward an object in the center of the crowd. At a closer look, the brothers could see that it was a lone puffer fish. Caspian pulled Noah further down the hallway and then whispered to him, "Remember I told you that the barracuda came up to us and spoke?" Noah nodded. "Peek out at the observation deck window. What does it look like to you?"

Carefully crawling, and peering around the corner, Noah looked. Then he retreated into the shadows of the hallway unseen by the crowd of animals outside of the ARK.

"It looks like the dolphins are all looking at the puffer fish? What's the big deal?" asked Noah.

"But why would they all be looking at the puffer fish. You know that dolphins don't eat puffer fish! They are hardly from the same oceanic zone. I think they are listening to it."

"Like the puffer fish is… is talking? Are you out of your mind?"

"Noah, since when have you known me to make up stories! I never play in on your pranks with Luke and Pac. I never even fib to Mom and Dad. Honestly, I heard that barracuda talk! Now look again and see if just maybe what I say could be possible."

Repeating his covert approach to the edge of the hallway and peeking around the corner, Noah looked again at the scene. And he could see that Caspian was right. The puffer fish was now pointing with its fin here and there, and the dolphins were looking and responding as humans do in conversation. Not ready to dive head first into the loony bin with his brother, Noah reluctantly admitted,

"I guess you could be right. They were looking left and right as the puffer fish pointed. But you know, dolphins have been known to provoke a puffer fish to the point of inflating, and then use it like a human would use a soccer ball."

"An entire pod of dolphins interested in one, deflated puffer fish? Think logically Noah." Caspian tried to rationalize.

"You mean logically like talking fish?" Noah shot back.

"Right. Okay, let's keep moving and see what else is going on here," Caspian said as he silently opened a sliding door.

Now out of the view of the observation deck, but not out of view of all windows, they continued to furtively move throughout the ARK. It seemed that the rest of their home remained unchanged. All laboratories and family pods were dark and unoccupied. For now, there was nothing else they could do. They traveled carefully through the ARK back to the kitchen and shared what they had seen with the others.

Huddled in the prepatory kitchen, they sat discussing their current situation. Their distance interfered with their ability to actually hear what was being said between the animals, but it was clear by their body language that they were in fact conversing.

"Why don't we just go swim out there and ask them what their damage is!?!" spouted off Pac.

"Lots of reasons," replied Sonora.

"Oh, yeah, like what?" Pac asked

"Well, for one, our parents took all but one of the SCUBA tanks. Second, if these animals could capture and detain a large group of full grown adults, imagine the possibilities of disaster if anyone of us faced them alone. If you need a third reason, I'm sure I could come up with one, but I think that those two reasons should be sufficient," Sonora said succinctly.

"Okay, so fine, going out there isn't an option," said Pac, refusing to be put out so easily. "So what *are* we going to do? I can't stand sitting around waiting anymore!" Pac whined.

"Ditto, dude," added Luke.

"Well the intelligent thing to do is think of a way to hear the information they are saying," said Stillman.

"Like what? A spy?" asked Pac.

"Well, yes, but one we can trust not to turn on us, no matter what," Stillman continued.

"What did you have in mind?" asked Luke interested, now that the subject of spying was on the table.

Chapter 24
Surface

It's a worm graveyard
On this shiny wet pavement
Worm-gut on my shoes
-A. Lee

Flynn discovered her dislike for water continued even while living on the surface. She avoided swimming pools, long showers, and most importantly, rain.

How incredibly unfair, she thought, *that one must have water doused upon them without a say in the matter. At least down there, being submerged under 10 quadrillion gallons of water, actually feeling wet was a choice. As long as I stayed in my room, or in the lab, then, at least then I was dry!*

Whenever it rained, Flynn sank into a dark mood. It was like little droplets ruining her new (supposedly dry) world one drip at a time. Drip, drip, drip. It had been raining for almost a week straight, which would easily explain Flynn's more than partly cloudy mood.

Another easy explanation could be that she hadn't heard from any one of her family members in quite a while. Caspian - nothing new. She didn't expect Mr. Water-for-brains to spare time from his highly important academic duties to call her. She knew his mind was occupied on all things scientific. It wasn't failing to hear from him that bothered her. It was that she hadn't heard from her neurotic, worry inclined parental units in more days than she cared to count.

The dropped transmission from Noah also continued to haunt her guilty conscience.

The rain continued to run streams down her window and her spirits continued to run downward along with them.

Walking from her last class to the activities board, she sank deeper and deeper into concern. Nora still had soccer practice. *Even in the rain?* Flynn thought. *Geez.*

Fallen leaves from the giant Banyan trees covered the parking lot like wallpaper, and the rain their paste to hold them in place. Flynn walked quickly through the curtain of rain, her fleece collar turned up and her shoulders hunched. She hadn't gotten used to the drastic temperature and weather changes. In the ARK everything was regulated. Temperature, air flow, lighting, daily schedules, everything!

The rain also meant that she would have to run inside today in the school's fitness center. The school fitness center is very nice, with up to date exercise equipment, but for Flynn it couldn't match running outside in the fresh air, with Luke's jangling leash keeping time with her footsteps. Running on a treadmill in the fitness center also meant other people being a part of a time she prized as her own. Something about showing off your sweatiness as a trophy for others to admire, the way some people did flaunting their glistening muscles, took away from the tranquil joy of pushing herself on her own terms.

So rain and fitness center it was. Two more reasons to be crabby, only adding to her already long list of complaints, including impending doom for her family and midterm exams next week.

After dinner, Nora walked into Flynn's room and found her in this distressing mood.

"What's with the brooding?" Nora asked.

"Reading the thesaurus again?" bit back Flynn, then stopped and smiled, welcoming Nora into the room.

"Well, Miss Smarty Pants, we didn't all grow up with genius scientists to aid our intellectual growth with a plethora of college prep vocabulary words. Some of us actually have to study to pass the SAT," Nora measuredly spit out taking a seat on the bed.

"Very impressive Miss Nelson, we here at the admissions board feel that you have great potential as a student at Wise Ass University," responded Flynn, tucking her legs up underneath her and turning towards Nora.

"Thank you very much. I learn from the best you know. So, really, what's your damage? You have been moping around for the past two days... maybe even three," Nora asked, taking her turn to be concerned.

"I don't know." Flynn sighed.

"Yes you do, you just don't want to admit it."

After a long pause, Flynn shook her head. "You're right. Man your intuitive power for human emotion is beyond scientific comprehension. Too bad they don't test that on the college entrance exams. You're right, You're right... I miss them," Curled up against the storm of mixed emotions inside her, she felt better just saying it out loud. She didn't feel embarrassed as tears crept up behind her eyes. She didn't have anything to hide from Nora.

"You think I don't understand? My family and I... way different. I mean seriously, a science prodigy and a beauty queen... my mom is a lab technician and my dad markets pro sports teams. We are as mixed a bag of nuts as there comes. I get it. No matter if you want to maim them one day, you know that someday, maybe not tomorrow, maybe not even next month, but someday, you will one day, like them."

"Maim, plethora, brooding? Wow, you have been studying."

"All right Miss Spokesperson for Cynics United, it's Friday night. We can't stay in. What do you say to some smoothies at the food court for refueling and then some quality time in the abundance of fabulous stores at the local mall, looking for outfits for tomorrow's party?"

"Now you're talking my language," Flynn said sliding off of the window seat and sliding her feet into flip flops.

And once again, the problems populating Flynn's mind

had been moved to the deeper and darker recesses of her brain… the section of her brain she reserved for things she wished to forget and no longer remember. But not to worry, these problems would not be lonely. There were memories of bad haircuts and an episode of food poisoning to keep the worry company.

Chapter 25
ARK

"People are people and sometimes it doesn't work out. Nothing we say is going to save us from the fall out." –Taylor Swift

They took turns doing nightly rounds every hour on the hour, always switching those who went out. They relied on the school of thought that each individual interprets a situation in a different way. The more ideas that they could collectively bring to the table, the better.

Carl and Stillman went out on the second round. Sonora and Nina on the third. Professor Bebee and Pac on the fourth. Luke and Anton on the fifth and then back to Caspian and Noah. While each team was out searching, the others slept, or tried to. Professor Bebee hacked continuously at her laptop and Nina poured through her Ocean Field guide until she thought her eyes were going to fall out. She was determined to find something useful. Eventually both fell asleep in their fruitless efforts, until it was their turn for rounds.

Caspian and Noah were on their way back to the inner kitchen when a bump against a fiber glass viewing window caused them to take the fetal position on the floor under the arch of a doorway. *Bump Bump. Bump bump bump.* After the third set of noises Caspian chanced a look up. It was the barracuda.

Caspian leapt from his hiding spot and pressed his hands and face to the window.

"What's going on?" he blurted out, forgetting that he was asking a fish for help.

"You are in danger," spoke the fish. Noah's jaw dropped and he too was pulled from his hidden location to the window, almost as if by magnetism. He could not believe what he had just heard.

"Yeah, we've gathered that much," whispered Caspian desperately. "But what is going on? What happened? Why can you talk and why can I understand you?"

"Too many questions for such a short time. For now, go to the kitchen, stay hidden, stay safe. And meet me here, at this spot again tomorrow at 8am."

"But..." Noah started to blurt out.

"Go, now. It isn't safe for either of us to talk right now. Go!" the barracuda severely instructed before quickly turning with a quick swish of his tail, and disappeared from the window.

Obediently, Noah and Caspian began their return trip to their hiding spot, moving faster, the fish's warning still fresh in their memory. As they rounded the corner to return, they heard shouting. Concerned, they picked up their pace, and were sickened at what they saw.

There was Luke, doing exactly what the barracuda had told them not to do. Luke was doing the opposite of hiding. He was out on the observational deck, shouting at a dolphin. As absurd as he looked, it was even more illogical when the dolphin responded.

"Look! We know we've messed up! That's why we're here! Can't you see that?" Luke shouted, tearing at his hair in frustration. "We're trying to fix things."

"Too little too late," the dolphin sternly replied.

"The damage your kind has done is irreparable. The temperatures are rising. The glaciers are melting. The water is polluted with garbage and the carcasses of dying animals due to your carelessness. It has gone on too long, and we will not stand for it any longer. It cannot be fixed and you must pay. If we left it up to you, we'd all die anyway, at least now it will be on our own terms."

"You sound ridiculous! Do you know that? We are

trying to fix it, so the pollution and the dying, and the rising temperatures, so it all stops! And you would just rather kill everything and everybody, quick and dirty, get it done?!?"

"End the suffering," the dolphin spoke again.

"Right, real rational you psycho!" Luke screamed through the window.

Professor Bebee put a hand on his shoulder and stepped forward. Incomprehensible as it might be, she was going to attempt to reason with, to rationalize, try to come to come to some solid ground of compromise with the talking sea creature she faced now. Her plea was simple for she knew it was unlikely to talk them out of taking any action. "Give us time. A year, 6 months. Let us try to make this right, and if we fail, you can take over."

There was not even a pause for thought.

"No," resounded the voice of the dolphin. "I - Adonis, leader of the pod and spokesperson for the Sea Clan tell you, humans, no."

"Spokesperson!" Pac shouted exasperated "Spokesperson! You are not even a person! You are…"

"Silence!" Adonis boomed. "We will leave you now. But know that you are being watched, and that we will be back." Then he turned, swam through a path that parted in the pod, and the others followed naturally, that is silently, without talking.

Chapter 26
Surface

"Nobody knows for certain what dreams tell us. They come to us at night and there is something dark about them. But they can also be as blinding as sunlight. The wise men say: Live your dream in sleep, but do not let your life become a sleep." – from <u>Zipporah, the Wife of Moses</u> *by Marek Halter.*

    Flynn awoke from a very weird dream. Oddly, there were mirrored moments from last night's double date. Maybe it was the movie theater popcorn and Milkdud combination that was to blame for the strange pairing of subjects in her dream. Alex and Nora had been there, and Flynn, of course.
    They were in the movie theater, sitting, chatting, playing the on screen trivia game that preceded the previews. And then suddenly, water began creeping down the aisles, and up to their ankles, past their knees, over their belly buttons... and try as hard as they might, they could not move. Their feet were frozen to the ground, their arms plastered to the arm rests. Stuck and drowning. When the water got up over their necks and flirted with covering their mouths, Flynn remembered shouting something. Her voice was strong, calm, not panicked as she expected it would sound. Totally in control. And at the sound of her commanding voice, the water vanished. She blinked and the four of them were sitting just as they had been before, none the wiser to the fact that they almost just drowned at the local Mega Plex 16.
    Glad that her eyes were open, and that she could hopefully forget the disturbing dream in the daylight, Flynn swung her feet out of the bed, sat up and took a deep breath. She scanned the room, taking a moment to fully wake up before standing up to start her day. Her eyes rested on two

envelopes sitting amongst a pile of homework and college admission pamphlets she had picked up from the guidance office (just in case her parents would entertain the idea of her going to college on the surface). Flynn reached over groggily and grabbed the first envelope.

The unmarked envelope had already been opened. Inside, in hasty scrawl it read-

Midterms this week. Fall break after that. No more packages for three weeks. Leave your lists on my desk at the Surface Station. I will fill your requests when I return.
- Simon

Her name was written on the second envelope in neat black ink on the front with the Nelson address below it, however, there was no return address in the left hand corner or stamp in the right hand corner. She slipped her perfectly polished finger under the sealed flap and opened the envelope. A letter written in the same inky black immaculate hand writing fluttered out of the envelope and onto the floor.

Flynn picked up the letter, crawled back under the covers and began to read.

Dear Flynn,

I know that we have never met, but I thought that after a couple of weeks to figure things out on your own in the ways of the world on the surface, I would write you, and offer some advice on maybe some of the things that may still be eluding you.

Nina. The letter is from Nina, Flynn thought.

But before I get to that, I would like to thank you for your restlessness (I am assuming that was the catalyst for your trip upward, I mean, I say assume after

I've talked to your family and the others down here). Without your desire to get out and see the surface world, I would never have gotten the incredible opportunity to live "in your shoes". The things I am learning, the experiences I am gaining, everything (maybe minus the dietary changes I've had to undergo — I've found I'm not one for seafood) have been amazing. More than I could ever imagine. So, thank you. Thank you a hundred times over.

Okay, so, I assume (not something I often do, except in this letter it seems, but distance in the communication will not allow otherwise) —

She has been hanging out with Caspian too much, Flynn thought. *She is beginning to write like he talks. The two together might be unbearable.* She was glad she was warm in her bed, and not down there sandwiched between the two of them for breakfast.

- that you have Mr. MaCan for Driver's Ed. You should know that he is legally blind in one eye. This information may be too little too late. Sorry. Hopefully you don't start your behind the wheel driving until later this Spring. But when you do, just be ready, because while he has an extra brake on his passenger side, the rumors are he has never used it in necessary situations. (Once to stop a sophomore from allegedly hitting a cat crossing the road, although no one else in the car actually saw that cat. And the jerky stop caused all the air bags in the car to go off, resulting in a one week hiatus in behind the wheel sessions for those attending Bay City High.)

The rest of the letter went on to describe a few more precautions Nina thought might be helpful to Flynn, including which bathroom at school never has a line and the fact that Mr. Bottleberke never locks the science lab. She also suggested a small ice cream shop about a mile from the Nelson's house that Flynn must visit before her time on the surface came to an end.

Nina ended the letter:

Fellow Life-Swapper,
Nina

Wow. Am I that self-centered? That I never thought to communicate with the girl who straight up traded lives with me? That I never spared a moment's thought about how she might be adjusting to life in the ARK? That all I have truly thought about up until now, is my hair color, my popularity, my future friends and boyfriend, me, me, me.

The reality of it kind of stung. And with the sting, came a desire to stay in bed, to think about the person she had become in the last two plus months, and if she really liked that person. The kind of person more concerned with shopping than her family's well-being. The kind of person who cared more about teenage drama shows than protecting the environment or cleaning up what mess was left of the environment. Had she really changed that much? Really, she thought that she had changed. And she wasn't sure she liked it. So in bed she stayed, until she could figure out exactly how she was going to make things right.

Chapter 27
ARK

"When you get to the end of your rope, tie a knot and hang on."
– Franklin Roosevelt

"This is more serious that we thought," Professor Bebee started once they were back in their safe hold. Sitting on counters, speechless, they stared at her. "We need to prepare for the worst." Everyone solemnly nodded in agreement. "The first thing we need to do is ensure our survival. I know that there are many other lives out there at stake, but we cannot do anything to help them if we ourselves are not alive. So first, we need to harvest what food remains in the ARK farm, and bring it back here to preserve. I'm not sure how long we will be staying down here, so might as well not take any chances of the crops being destroyed before we can benefit from them. Carl, Anton and Nina, I'd like you three to take that job. I can help with the preservation once you get back."

Silently their team of three got up to leave, but before they could make it to the door, Professor Bebee added one more instruction, "I know that before, we were operating under secrecy, but that is not our highest priority anymore. Survival is. Be as stealthy as possible, but do what you have to do to get that food back here. If that means being seen, so be it." They nodded again and then left, several tan canvas bags in hand.

"Luke, Pac and Noah, de-salinify as much water as possible. Go down to the Obscoral tank. I know it will break your heart to drain your playground, but surely you understand our situation? And besides, it would take months to go through its entire supply. So I highly doubt your sports sanctuary will be completely run dry." Noah both pouted and nodded before he slid off the counter and went to do as he was told.

"Caspian and I are going to work in the communication lab to try and figure out why we are not able to reach the Surface Station, which leaves you, Sonora and Stillman, our remaining animal specialists, to do a search for any and all useful information on animal mutation. Search the university research archives and the zoological society data base."

While Caspian and Professor sat down to the computers in the communication lab, and were waiting for the programs to open, Caspian said, "Too bad Flynn isn't here. She was queen of the tech lab castle. We could really use her expertise right now." Professor Bebee nodded silently in agreement. After a few more moments of silence passed Caspian spoke again. "I can see why they picked you."

"Picked me for what?" Professor Bebee asked

"To be a part of the ARK project. I know that there was no question even close to this on the application and interview process. You know, 'what to do in impending doom?' But they must have seen how brilliant you would be in the answers you gave to all the other questions they did ask. I'm glad you're here."

"Well, Caspian, I wish none of us were here, but I understand what you are trying to say. And I thank you. Now, what do you say we get to work?"

And so they did. They seemed to have power, but for some reason, their video conferencing capabilities were cut. A blank and silent screen reflected their worried faces. Scarier than the malfunctioning technology was the fact that no one on the surface seemed to notice their missing presence. How could they not know that something had gone horribly wrong, let alone changed? How could they not know? How could they seriously not know?

Because the animals had not taken their attack to land. Yet.

Chapter 28
Surface

"If pleasures are greatest in anticipation, just remember that this is also true of trouble." – Elbert Hubbard

Saturday had passed in many self-loathing hours without communication from anyone in the ARK. Not even several trips around the block with Luke loyally running beside her, leash dangling between them, was enough to chase away the guilt.

Flynn waited all day in her room for her converter to buzz to life. She even tried a few times to call down to the ARK herself. But no one was answering. The dream, the self-degradation, the lack of response that she so desperately wanted now... Flynn added them all up to an equation of bad karma. She knew she deserved it, but that didn't make the taste of her own bitter medicine any easier to swallow.

It turned out that getting out of bed on Friday had been totally worth it. At lunch, she returned to her regular lunch table, tray filled with a salad and French fries, to find Alex sitting making small talk with her new friends.

"Hey, can I steal you away for a minute?" he asked as she approached the table.

"Yeah, sure," Flynn answered, way calmer than she actually felt. Alex stood and led her around a corner, just out of view from the majority of the lunch room.

"I'm sorry I have to do this now, but I have soccer practice right after school... so it's now, or in social studies, or not at all."

"Okay," said Flynn, more of a question than a statement.

"I just wanted to know if you would be my date to

Savannah's party tomorrow night," he asked her confidently.

"Yes. That would be great."

"Awesome."

"But,"

"But..?" he paused. "Oh, did you not have a good time the other night? You don't have to say yes. I mean, don't feel obligated."

"No, it's not that. I just, ah, don't want to cause trouble, that's all," Flynn explained, examining her choices through a new lens since her soul searching that morning.

"Trouble?" Alex asked, confused.

"For you. For Savannah."

"Seriously, Flynn, don't worry about it."

"Really?"

"Really."

"Okay, then yes, I'd love to go."

"Great. Now the uncool part. I don't drive yet. Can I meet you there?"

"Sure, I'll get a ride and spot you a few cool points."

"Awesome. Now go eat your lunch. That is if any of your fries are left. Knowing your friends, I highly doubt it."

"No worries. See you tomorrow."

"Can't wait."

They went their separate ways, both smiling, both looking forward to the party even more than before (if that was even possible for Flynn, which she highly doubted).

Now, Saturday night had found her, and despite her personal quandary, she couldn't help but be excited. Whatever was going on down there, she was sure it could wait until Sunday. What could possibly happen in 36 hours? It was only 36 hours.

The 36 hours she was postponing a guilty conscience of moral and family obligation - was the 36 hours that she had been looking forward to for her whole life. *Her first party.*

Chapter 29
ARK

"There are no extra pieces in the universe. Everyone is here because he or she has a place to fill, and every piece must fit itself into the big jigsaw puzzle." – Deepka Chopra

The night passed slowly. 8:00am came, blinking on Caspian's light up watch face. It seemed bright, in comparison to the semi-dark space of the preparatory kitchen. The beeping alarm caused those sleeping near him to stir, but as he silenced the alarm and got up to leave, they settled back into their sleeping bags, resuming their sleep. Usually by eight o' clock, things in the ARK would be in full swing, breakfast being eaten, plans for the day being made, labs being scheduled. But not today. Due to their worried talks late into the night, they were all still soundly asleep.

After their confrontation with the dolphins yesterday, the meeting with the barracuda was paramount. Caspian still couldn't wrap his scientific brain around the whole situation. How on earth could this have happened? Which in Caspian's head sounded more like: *Under what chemical combinations and theories is something like this plausible?*

Careful not to disturb the others as he tiptoed over their sleeping bodies, he picked his way precariously toward the door into the dining room, hoping that the fish would have helpful information, or even just a shred of reasoning behind the whole preposterous situation.

He didn't have to wait long. Crossing the dining room quickly, and low to the ground, he slipped out the side entrance and worked his way down to the docking station, where the barracuda had asked to meet.

By the time Caspian arrived, the fish was already there

waiting for him.

He wasn't sure if it was entirely possible, but the fish looked tired. Caspian couldn't pin point the features that led him to this conclusion, and he knew scientifically speaking that fish didn't sleep, but somehow, he still knew it to be true. The fish, unknowingly to Caspian thought the same thing of him.

"Looks like nobody got much sleep last night," the barracuda said

"You sleep?" Caspian asked, vocalizing his internal question of moments before.

"Never mind, it's not important. We have much more imperative things to discuss right now."

"Agreed," Caspian said with a nod, and then continued. "Do you have any idea how this happened or what is going on? How far has this, this" he struggled to come up with a word to encompass the images he had seen in the last twenty four hours, "this *situation* spread?"

"Whoa, one question at a time. And I am not promising I have all the answers, but I will tell you what I know."

"Why?"

"I am not entirely sure, but I know that returning things to normal, the way they were, is the lesser of two evils, even with the threat of global warming, melting glaciers and pollution. I know that what they have planned, will probably be worse than that… and we'd probably all end up in the same place anyway. So, I've picked my side, and you're it."

"Okay," sighed Caspian, shocked by the complex thought pattern of the scaled animal that he once pictured only as something to study, or eat. "So, first question, how did this happen?"

"I think that will be our most difficult question to answer, so I will start out with what I know. The earliest memories I have, those beyond my 15 second fish memory, started two days ago, in the mid-morning. The sunlight was just beginning to filter down, as low as we are. It was instant. It was as if a wave of comprehension and knowledge washed over me with the passing tide, and I was changed."

"Wait! Two days ago?" a wave of comprehension suddenly hit Caspian too. "The PE-328."

"Excuse me?" asked the barracuda.

"The PE-328. It is a pollution eating compound that we have created. We have been trying to produce a chemically safe agent to release into the water to increase the speed of the degradation of garbage and pollution that has found its way into the ocean."

"And this – chemical solution – they released it into the water two days ago?"

"Exactly. They left at 10:30am, and most likely released the potion near eleven, which would coincide with your memories of the time your change took place."

"Okay, so now, we know the how, or at least, the basic of the how, if not the specific. This is what else I can tell you…"

They continued to discuss in the safety of their cove underneath the shelter of the loading dock, hidden away from the prying eyes of the sea creatures.

Chapter 30
Surface

"Take a look who just walked in, and she didn't come alone. I can't stand to see this. Someone take me home." – Plain White T's

Again Flynn found herself in the middle of a moment that before she could only dream of. But at this moment she was not dreaming, she was riding in a car. The car, well actually a minivan, was being driven by Mr. Nelson to a party. A real, live, actual party. Flynn found it difficult to sit still and control her urge to squeal in excitement.

When the minivan door rolled open and Flynn stepped onto the driveway of Savannah's house, she had to remind herself not to hyperventilate. When she looked up and saw Alex leaning against the porch railing, she had to remind herself to breathe.

Smiling his beautiful smile from the lighted porch, he watched her walk towards the house. Together, hand in hand, they walked into the house.

No one paid particular attention to Flynn, Alex and Nora as they walked in. (Except for Riley, Nora's boyfriend, who found Nora and was likewise glued to her general vicinity for the rest of the night). But as the night wore on, accounts of Flynn and Alex's hand holding and laughing and dancing made their way to Savannah. Let's just say that she was less than amused. Losing her object of affection was definitely not on her birthday wish list. She decided she needed to do something about it.

Savannah's house was located on a beautiful bay lot, with the luxury of a backyard beach. Although the fishy aroma was overpowering at times, no one could deny the awesomeness of the view. It was on the beach by the bonfire that Savannah found Flynn and Alex sitting close, laughing at a joke Riley had just told.

If looks could kill, Savannah's would have been a massacre. Flynn felt the stare before she saw it. Flynn looked up and wished she hadn't. She squeezed Alex's hand, and he too met Savannah's lethal gaze. Alex opened his mouth to say something, but he didn't get the chance.

Chapter 31
ARK

"The thing I hate about an argument is that it always interrupts a discussion." – G.K. Chesterton

Caspian found the others in different stages of waking up. Stretching, yawning, rolling up their sleeping bags, getting ready for a day that held they knew not what. He came in quietly, not wanting to startle anyone. Everyone had jittery nerves after the past couple days.

He wandered over to a counter, where some of the food they had gathered, but had yet to store was laying out. Caspian grabbed a granola bar, took a bite, and then realized that everyone in the room was staring at him.

"Soooooo, what did Mr. Fish say?" Pac asked.

"Actually he likes to be called 'Cuda." Caspian started as he slowly chewed.

"Oh…sure," said Pac, not sure whether or not he should apologize.

"'Cuda and I went over the facts, and this is our conclusion. The change from instinct based floating animal to humanesque reasoning creature happened simultaneously with the release of the PE-328. We deduced this due to the approximate times both incidents occurred."

Nina still struggled sometimes to decode Caspian's scientific talk. But that's part of what she liked so much about him… his raw knowledge and his ability to figure things out, in a way and speed that surpassed anyone else she knew. Granted, most other guys she knew used their abilities to master X-Box, so her comparison wasn't really all that fair. Still, he won hands down. She smiled at him, and he continued.

"He told me something else. They have the others. Our parents. Adonis and the other creatures, they have them hidden away somewhere, guarded. But they are alive."

"Where?!?" Sonora shouted, beginning to breathe quickly. It was a subject they had avoided talking about. But now that the topic had surfaced again, it was like ripping off an industrial strength band-aid. The pain was fresh and raw.

"He doesn't know. They aren't saying, because fish like 'Cuda are still around. They haven't managed to recruit everybody, I mean every creature to their side." Caspian explained.

"Well we have to find them!" Noah shouted.

"I know, but how?" Caspian asked.

"We should leave." Anton said.

"I'm sorry, are you lacking oxygen?" Luke accused. "Leave? Did you hear him? Our parents are out there... alive... somewhere!"

"Yeah, I heard him. Glad his informant was so specific. We should go to the surface, get the other scientists to help. We can't do this on our own!" Anton justified.

"Do you really think that anyone up there is even going to believe us? I mean, talking sea creatures! How exactly do you plan to prove it to them?" Pac asked.

"And besides, it takes months of funding and planning for those Surface Station scientists to actually do anything productive," added Sonora

"Now now." Professor Bebee stepped in. "I will not have my fellow colleagues slandered in this event, of which they are completely unaware. However, I do agree with Anton."

"No! No no no! You are wrong! Forgive me Professor, but we need to stay, we can't just leave them!" Caspian shouted in a rare moment of hysterics.

"I am sorry Caspian, and to you too, Luke, Pac, Sonora, to whomever believes we should stay. I feel our only move is to go up. Our supplies are limited as is our ability to move freely within even the ARK, not to mention the outer capacity of the water surrounding the ARK is restrained. We need more resources to search for the others."

"You mean later. Who knows how much later... and it could be too LATE!" Pac roared.

Noah and Nina sat silently by, letting the more experienced hash it out, not knowing for themselves which side they would take if they were in the decision maker's shoes. Suddenly the race was on.

"I'm going up. Whoever is coming with me, better come now. I'm not waiting for the rest of the circus to come to town and set up shop." And with that Anton turned, and ran to the loading dock. The others exchanged panicked looks before racing after him.

Fueled by the heat of the argument, Luke and Anton made it to the Tube first. Expecting shouts and shoves, Professor Bebee entered the room last to complete silence. To their surprise the Tube was inoperable. It was blocked. Blocked to the point of no use. Several hundred puffer fish swam in the passage way of the Tube, blocking the flow of water, that when pressurized would send the Tube up or down. For the moment the fish swam around freely, but at will, they could inflate and make movement, small or large, impossible.

"Well," said Professor Bebee cutting the thick silence, "it looks like nobody is going anywhere. At least not right now." She sighed loudly. "Alright, back to the kitchen, it seems we have some things to discuss and plan for. Obviously we are going to be thinking long term from here on out."

Chapter 32
Surface

"I am slowly falling apart and I wish you'd take a walk in my shoes for a start. You might think it's easy being me... you just stand still look pretty." – The Wreckers

"So let me get this straight." Savannah began, making herself the center of attention. "You arrive on the Bay City scene, become instantly popular, claim not to shower, are smarter than the teachers and no one seems to care?"

No one dares to move, lest the wrath and fury of Savannah find them as her next target.

"I am so tired of everything in the past two months being about you. You come to my house for my birthday party. And what is everyone talking about? You! You and my ex-boyfriend. Well I am not going to stand for it anymore. I'm going to do something about it!" she raved, walking now around the circle, matching her ferocious gaze with those sitting around the bonfire. "I am going to do something that everyone will be talking about."

Then Savannah turned and began walking toward the water. She kicked off one flip flop and then the other. As she passed a group of boys playing Frisbee in the peripheral glow of the fire, she pushed one roughly to the ground and kissed him full on the mouth. She didn't care who it was, she just wanted people to see it and then to talk about it. A lot.

To add the icing to her dramatic spectacle, she then ran off toward the bay and jumped into the cool night water.

"Umm, does she know that dusk is feeding time for sharks?" asked Flynn.

Someone screamed. Instantly there was a mad dash to the shoreline. After searching for ten minutes with no more a trace of Savannah than her slender footprints, someone thought to go get Savannah's mom. Naturally she freaked out and called the police.

The only clue, Savannah's footprints, were now nonexistent because dozens of teenagers walking up and down the beach had now put their mark on the scene. Friends searched. Social enemies searched. Parents searched. Neighbors searched. The police searched. No one found Savannah.

Chapter 33
ARK

"A woman is like a teabag. You never know how strong she is until you drop her in hot water." ~ Nancy Reagan

    Professor Bebee took control immediately, evaluating the situation and issuing orders.

    "Our options are dwindling. We must rely on ourselves from now on. We must concentrate on the four most important tasks to us right now. We will need to continue to harvest the food from the gardens, stock what remaining dried foods and fresh seafood we have. In the next few days we should also consider replanting what we have taken. It would be a shame to last longer than our food supply. We can't beat anyone, if we starve to death first. We will also need to check our water supply and continue to desalinify and store as much as possible. Nina, Noah, you will be responsible for those jobs."

    "But-" Noah started to protest, but after a quick look from Professor Bebee, he closed his mouth and sulked silently. *Anyone but her*, he thought. *Couldn't I work with anyone but her?*

    "Luke and Pac. You and your WakeTecs will be searching the area just outside the ARK for the others. Search as well as you can without invoking the wrath of Adonis or whatever he has chosen to call himself. Be safe, but do what you do best, be sneaky. We have to find them."

    Changing the direction of her gaze she looked next to Stillman and Sonora. "You two, along with myself will be working on the PE-328, trying to figure out went wrong, trying to reverse it."

    "And what about us?" Caspian asked pointing to himself, Anton and Carl.

"You three will be working on the communication system, and try to solve our connection problem, or lack of connection to be specific. Even if we are not going to the surface for help, doesn't mean we can't be in contact with them for assistance."

"Alright. Let's get started. We will meet back here in three hours to report your progress and eat lunch," Professor Bebee commanded.

The group split into their small factions to dutifully follow the given instructions. Shock, anger and fear aside, they were determined to survive.

Chapter 34
Surface

"You can't unscramble scrambled eggs." – Meet Joe Black

An hour of unsuccessful searching had passed and the party had been officially called off. All kids had been sent home and now only the police and coast guard remained in the search for the missing Savannah Lynn Taylor.

Flynn and Nora had lain awake in Nora's room, though Mrs. Nelson thought them asleep long ago. Their brains moved too quickly with possible scenarios, things said that night, and crowding in with all those thoughts, substantial amounts of guilt.

"If I weren't here, none of this would have happened," worried Flynn.

"You don't know that for sure. Savannah has pulled stunts like this before. It's all a game," Nora said.

"Yeah, but the stuff with Alex."

"No. Stop. Flynn, this is not your fault. She did a stupid thing. A stupid, jealousy motivated, thing. That now, she can't un-do."

"Nora?"
"Yeah?"
"Do you think she's dead?"
"I don't know. I… I don't know. Let's just go to sleep."
"Nora?"
"Yes Flynn?"
"Thank you for being my friend."
"I'm glad you came. This year wouldn't have been the same without you."

And so the friends' conversation ended, but they did not go to sleep. Silently Flynn pondered the thoughts in her own mind. *What was going to happen? Where did she go? What if she really is dead? Will they say it's my fault? Who was that boy that she kissed? I wonder if Alex can sleep.*

Finally, mercifully, sleep found them and they drifted off into the current of unmemorable dreams.

Chapter 35
Unknown Waters outside the ARK

"Impossible is a word to be found only in the dictionary of fools." – Napoleon Bonaparte

It was true that Savannah's parents and the police and the rest of Bay City did not know where she was. They worried day and night about her supposed disappearance. But lost, did not accurately describe Savannah's situation.

In fact, she had been found. No, she had not been found by sharks feeding in the shallow waters at dusk. She was found by a pod of dolphins that had been doing reconnaissance work near the Surface Station. The dolphins' super sensitive hearing picked up the noises of the birthday party and Savannah's drama queen entrance into the bay did not go unnoticed. They seized the opportunity to take another hostage.

Yes, another hostage. The dolphins already had eleven other hostages. The ARK scientists, gone missing, were also not so much missing, as detained. They took Savannah quickly, before she could become oriented and fight their pull of her underwater. They swam down, diving deep into the water, each grabbing a portion of her shirt in their bottle nose mouths. Dragging her down into the water. Deeper and deeper. In their descent with her, she lost consciousness near their destination.

Their arrival came just in time, leaving a window of life for Savannah to crawl back through, if her body was strong enough. They stopped with her rag-doll-like body in front of a small dome, a mini version of the ARK. One of the dolphins tapped its nose on the window and when the faces of the scientists appeared said, "Come, claim one of your own, before it dies."

    Though they did not recognize her, they scrambled to retrieved Savannah's body immediately. Someone quickly performed CPR, and helped her to dispel the large amounts of water in her lungs and stomach. Then she was put to bed and wrapped in blankets to bring her body temperature back to normal. They took turns watching over her, puzzling over who she was, how the dolphins had captured her, and as they had been talking of since they found themselves prisoners… they talked of the meaning behind these strange, strange events.

Chapter 36
ARK

"I cannot discover that anyone knows enough to say definitely what is not possible." – Henry Ford

Are you kidding me!? Are you kidding me!!?! Caspian paced, a habit he knew familiar to his sister. He wished she were pacing now instead of him. He wished she had any concern toward the situation at hand at all. *No,* thought Caspian. *This has moved beyond a situation. This is a catastrophe. A brilliant error of design. A scientific nightmare. But is she concerned? No! Instead she is shopping, dyeing her hair, gallivanting off on dates, hell who knows what stupid girly mundane surface activity she is up to! But for Poseidon's sake! We have a crisis here.*

"Dang it Flynn, pick up your converter!" Caspian shouted into the small rectangular device he held in his shaking hand. If they couldn't use the computer system within the ARK to communicate with the surface station, then they would have to rely on their hand held communication device, the converter, which was pretty much a fancy high-tech walkie-talkie that could do a whole lot more than transfer voices over a long distance. But that was the only function that Caspian currently cared about, the part that let him talk to his presently estranged sister.

Nina watched nervously from the arm chair that they had dragged into the kitchen. She was biting her nails, and once she realized it, she took to wringing her hands. And when that did not expend enough nervous energy, she took to pacing too. Professor Bebee, Sonora, Carl and Anton were stationed in various corners of the kitchen either too tired or mentally drained to move much.

This was where Pac and Noah found them. Pacing.

Back and forth. Back and forth.

"You two worry warts are worse than a crossing guard after school. Back and forth, back and forth," Noah said shaking his head.

"Do you think pacing is going to clear the tubes? Do you think pacing is going to get things back to normal? Pacing- going to send these… mutant creatures back to the numb brain place they came from?" Pac scolded, half way between a lecture and a pep talk. "Now Luke, Noah and I," he continued, "have been doing a bit more than pacing." In the face of a lecture, the rest of them did not have even enough energy to groan. They continued to sit in their silence, ready to listen and take what was to come, in whatever tone it was delivered. "We came up with a plan."

At the mention of a plan their heads perked up and looked to Pac, ready for him to describe their idea. With that signal from his crew members he began to dramatically tell them of what he hoped to be a big successful step in the right direction toward ending this madness.

"Okay, this is what we came up with. We're gonna round up a school of sea snakes and release 'em into the Tube." He did not let the exasperated looks from Caspian and Professor Bebee stop him, instead he pressed on, "We thought about it while we were out riding today, avoiding all the fish."

"I thought there was only one SCUBA tank?" asked Nina.

"There was, and we took turns using it. We also used some of the emergency ventilator packs and attached them to our goggles," Pac explained "It actually worked pretty well."

"But Pac," Sonora yelled, "those are for emergencies!"

"Sonora, what exactly do you think qualifies as an emergency, if not this?" Stillman shot back. Sonora slumped back in to her chair and nodded for Pac to continue.

"Anyway, so some of the creatures helped us. We thought that if some fish helped us today, there are bound to be more out there."

"But how do we know who will help us and who won't? I mean before we get eaten?" asked Anton

"Just give us a minute to explain, dude! We looked through our Sea Guide and found that sea snakes are one of the few natural enemies of puffer fish," Pac said. "There is a school currently taking refuge in the upper canopies of the League of the Dark Vines. 'Cuda told me so. And Caspian, I totally apologize for not believing you. Talking fish?! Who would have thought? Wicked cool I mean, did you know-"

"Pac!" Caspian interrupted, "The plan?"

"Here's the deal. If we can get them to join us, we will help bring them to the ARK and release them at the right time into the Tube. Once we release 'em, they will attack the puffer fish, getting them to deflate and high tail it in the opposite direction, that being up" Pac said pointing in the same direction. "The surface."

"Best case scenario: they rise too quickly. It will create bubbles in their blood and they will die. Our second chance is that they will be attacked by the sea snakes, be infected with their venom and die. The sea snakes will then, carefully, slowly, make their way to the surface, exit the end of the Tube in the Surface Station, slither back to the water and be on their merry way," said Luke.

"Either way, we should buy ourselves some time for the Tube to ascend and allow Flynn to travel down with supplies and hopefully some help." When Pac finished, he looked expectantly at the rest of them, hoping they saw few if any flaws in their plan, and also hoping that they were crazy enough to venture into the League of the Dark Vines to find the sea snakes. By the end of their plan explanation Pac was pacing too, although probably more from excitement than worry.

It was Nina who spoke first, "Not be a complete fool, but could someone please give me a brief background on sea snakes?"

"No problem dear," said Professor Bebee with all the impeccable manners of an English tea party. "No time like the present for a little pop quiz. Sonora, darling, could you please inform Miss Nelson about sea snakes?"

"Of Course Professor Bebee." And then turning to Nina she said, "Sea snakes, especially the ones around here, are incredibly poisonous. Their poison can cause nausea, paralysis, kidney failure and even death. They are one of the few aquatic air breathing invertebrates. They live in shallow waters and near islands. They are small, less than a meter long. The sea snakes who live near the ARK and travel between here and Hawaii annually are called yellow bellied sea snakes."

"And we want to go and FIND these sea snakes?" Nina asked horrified.

"Alright, alright," said Caspian in a tone of resignation. "Suppose we were mentally unbalanced enough to leave the safety of the ARK to go to the League of the Dark Vines, and that by sheer miracle we are not poisoned to death by the sea snakes themselves, and they agree to help us and clear the Tube, how is Flynn supposed to know to enter the Tube and bring supplies? I mean, it's not exactly as if she is open to communication at this point," he said waving the non-responding converter in the air for all to see.

"She knows, because I just emailed her. Well, emailed Nora, care of Flynn," said Luke as he stepped around the corner making a dramatic entrance. "Funny we never thought of it before. Actually we used Nina's account to email her sister. Sorry Nina," he said looking now in her direction. "One flaw of living with scientists' kids is that we know a lot about computers and how to get around passwords."

"I'll forgive you," said Nina smiling.

"We will wait to hear from her again before we set up a plan to meet the sea snakes," Pac said very diplomatically.

And then, "Well, what do you think? Can we pull it off?"

Professor Bebee was the one to answer this time and said, "Well, if ever there was a lot that could do it, we'd be it." And as if motivated by their professor's courage and faith in them, they began to discuss in detail just how they would carry into action the plan set before them.

"It could work," Caspian said coming down from his rage.

"What do you mean it could work?" said Luke exasperated. "It's a genius plan. And one you can't even doubt it because it didn't come from the brilliant Brinestone family tree! Because it did."

Caspian looked up from his head hung position, confusion written clearly on his face. Understanding reached him when he saw Noah give him a thumbs up sign.

"Alright little brother!" Caspian said jumping up. After high fiving Noah on his way out the pod doorway, he bee-lined out of the kitchen. The rest of the remaining crew jumped up and immediately followed him. Nina caught up with him first.

"Hey! Hey! Where are you going?" she asked, slowing her jog to a quick walk to finally fall into stride with Caspian as he walked into his family pod.

"To get this," Caspian confirmed as he held up the glass mermaid figurine that Nina had carefully stowed away in a box with tissue in a desk drawer. She had packed up most of Flynn's possessions by this time, out of respect or disgust, Nina couldn't quite decipher which emotion was stronger. But she had definitely remembered this particular item she packed away. She took it from Caspian's hand and began to examine it in the beam of her flashlight.

"Why this?" Nina asked.

"We'll take a picture of it and include it in the next email. Because if Flynn sees this, it will show her how serious this whole thing actually is. It will show her how much we need her help, show her that we aren't playing around down here, that everyone really is gone and most importantly, that we need her help."

Chapter 37
Surface

"My stupid mouth, got me in trouble. I said too much again."
– John Mayer

It was in Nora's 4th hour study hall before lunch that she got the email from Nina's account. She had gotten a pass from study hall to go to the computer lab to type up her composition essay on <u>Farewell to Arms</u> for English Literature. Actually, students were forbidden to check email within the school, but Nora, feeling rebellious in the stifling monotony of her daily schedule, and just plain sick of the wordiness of Hemingway, not to mention looking for an escape of any thoughts related to the missing Savannah, chanced a peek.

Keeping one eye on the study hall monitor and the other on her computer screen, she quickly pulled up her Gmail account, typed in the password and waited impatiently for her inbox screen to appear. Immediately an email whose message was entitled: HELP!! URGENT!! FLYNN AND NORA!! grabbed her attention.

Two mouse clicks and the message was open. Quickly she copied and pasted the information to a Word document. She opened one other email with the same title in the subject line. It was a picture. She copied the picture and also put it on the Word document. Then she exited the email account and took a closer look at what the emails said. Apparently, Nina and her new friends were in trouble, big trouble. But she didn't quite understand it all.

Nora glanced to the study hall monitor again, and seeing that her nose was deep in a book, Nora saved and then printed the document. Casually, Nora stood, walked to the single lab printer and retrieved the papers. Walking quickly back to her seat, Nora put the papers into her satchel backpack and fidgeted away the last eleven minutes of study hall. No way could she go back to her essay now.

At the bell, Nora was a blur of motion out the door and down the hall to find Flynn. She found her almost at once exiting math. Nora grabbed her wrist, muttered something about eating out for lunch and dragged her down the hallway and out a side door. They walked hurriedly through the parking lot, across the soccer field and to a bench under a tree. Before Flynn could even mutter a syllable, Nora shoved the papers into her hands and waited in an unnerved silence for some information.

Flynn held the crumpled papers in her hands, wetting them with the sweat from her hands. Her eyes raced across the page as she drank in the words. Thoughts crowded her mind until it felt so full that she thought they would start spilling out of her ears. Seeing clearly was difficult. She was glad she was sitting down. The slight breeze was nice too. It seemed as if someone had pressed the mute button on her life. And then, it all came out at once. An explosion of words and emotion. At first it was difficult for Nora to understand Flynn through the ranting and shouts of angst (thanks Hemingway and SAT prep for that word thought Nora).

Flynn, now up from the bench and wearing a path through the grass with her flip flops, suddenly turned to Nora and shouted, "Do you know what this means?"

Trying to remain calm Nora answered, "Kind of, but not entirely. Together we must be able to do something to help. It can't be impossible."

"Can't be impossible!?! Can't be impossible!!" ranted Flynn. "You know Nora, sometimes you are a dumb blonde. Did you even read this email?"

"For your information, I did. If you would look past the end of your own nose you would see that I am trying to help! Maybe if I am just a dumb blonde then I can't possibly understand you and your cataclysmic disaster. Maybe I should just go to lunch and leave you and your big brain to solve this all on your own."

In a speed that would make Beckham jealous, Nora ran back to school. Flynn, realizing she had just knocked the legs out from under the one person on earth (or underwater) who really understood her, sank back onto the bench. Flynn balled up her knees to her chest and buried her face in them, and for the first time since arriving to the surface she cried.

The email fluttered from her hands and settled onto the grass below the bench.

Flynn and Nora,

Don't beat yourself up about totally blowing us off. I'm serious. It's prolly my fault for pullin' your chain so many times before. But that doesn't completely let you off the hook... We are in big trouble. Trouble does not even begin to describe what we are in.

A week and a half ago, the adults released the PE-328. Attached are the chemical components of it and its molecular map. (See if your genius brain sees something they overlooked... a side effect, a mutation, something... anything). Less than twelve hours after its release, all of the adults (except for Professor Bebee) went out to poke around and check things out.

They never came back. Sorry for the dramatics, but really that is what happened. We were all pumped at first, and had a killer time around the ARK, doing everything we aren't supposed to do. Like running with scissors, kidding, but eventually we figured out that stuff was pretty screwed up. First of all, the animals, they can talk. They can think. Not kidding. No jokes Flynn, Poseidon's honor.

The dolphins are the ring leaders, it seems. They have corrupted several sea creatures to go against us. We are like prisoners in the ARK. There is always someone (well something if you want to be technical) watching us. Those creatures that haven't gone against us remain hidden in fear. But they are lurking about too.

I know this all sounds confusing Flynn, but try to believe us. We need your help. There is still more to tell you. Caspian will fill you in tonight. Be by your converter at 7:00 tonight. Caspian will be calling you then. Please, you are our only life line.

~Luke

Underneath the letter was the second page that Nora had printed off. It was the mermaid's eyes that looked up at Flynn when she finally stopped crying and picked up the papers. She started trudging back toward the school, hoping that sometime before 7:00pm a brilliant plan would find its way to her brain. An equally large part of her was also hoping she would find a gesture grand enough that would act as an apology to Nora.

Chapter 38
ARK

"Perhaps all the dragons of our lives are princesses who are only waiting to see us once beautiful and brave." – Rainer Maria Rilke

Waiting for the time to call Flynn and Nora was near torture. But luckily they had plenty to keep both their hands and minds occupied. With the adult scientists out of the ARK, there were less people to complete the daily maintenance tasks, so it fell to the kids to pick up the slack and get the chores done. They continued to manage the ARK farm and gardens, harvesting the food, and planting more crops. Water was constantly being purified and stored. But amongst the mundane chores, another, more exciting event was taking place in the prepatory kitchen where the most senior members of the remaining crew were hard at work.

Maps covered every available flat surface. Pencils flew, calculations were made, opinions were voiced. What was the best way to reach the League of the Dark Vines? A straight shot, and risk being seen? A roundabout route, and risk running into something worse than the dolphins? What if there were scouts? Or spies? These were the questions they battled, facing each one head on, knowing that no question was too big or too scary to shy away from, because their lives depended on it.

Lives. Their lives. Their parents' lives. When had science ever asked this much of them? Would they have come down to the ARK in the first place if they knew they would have to potentially pay this price?

And deep in the ARK, below the main levels was Carl, checking over the SQUID, preparing it for its biggest mission ever. He oiled all external extremities, making sure each arm moved with expert precision. He checked the engine, and air pumps. He cleaned out any unnecessary supplies from the past missions, and stocked the traveling compartments with anything and everything that might be helpful, including the antidote to sea snake poison. *Gotta be prepared for everything. Although why we are preparing for this, insanely impossible road trip is still beyond me at this point. Majority rules, sucks when you are the minority.* But he continued working. He knew that in their little scientific community, the more brains the better, and sometimes when it came to making a decision, your preferred plan of action wasn't always the one chosen, someone else's plan was. Usually if the first plan failed, you got to use your plan next, or eventually, depending on the number of proposed plans. *Just sucks that if this plan fails, I probably won't have the opportunity to try my plan, because I'll be dead on the side of the road. What an adrenaline waste.*

Finally, he updated the GPS, and would soon program the route those upstairs were planning. *Hope they know what they are doing. Or we are all fish food.*

Fortunately, or unfortunately, depending on your view, time was ticking by and they wouldn't have to wait much longer to hear from the girls on the surface. Then, they'd put the plan into action.

Chapter 39
Surface

"You can't judge people by the things they done. You judge them by what they are doing." – Because of Winn Dixie (Kate DiCamillo)

The idea came to her on a run. She had left school as early as possible to get out for some fresh air. She took Luke (the dog) for some company. Animals had a calming effect on her. A dog and a run. This was her self-prescribed therapy. And it worked.

While on her return trip back to the house on Lakeshore Drive, the idea came to her. Why hadn't they thought of him before? After all he was the man behind it all. The mastermind. Then she, and he, could come down with supplies and help. Although what supplies and help she would bring was still a mystery, but still a plan was forming.

She was almost feeling back to normal as she jogged up the Nelson driveway, opened the front door and walked into the house, just in time to see Nora coming down the stairs. Suddenly, her exercise euphoria melted away leaving only a puddle of guilt.

Flynn and Nora went through the actions of their afternoon, without enthusiasm. Avoiding each other when possible, making excuses not to be near one another. To put it bluntly, it was one of Flynn's not so hot days since arriving to the surface. Eventually family dinner was over and they could go their separate ways without being obligated to share the same space.

The internet, a seemingly endless source of information, was not yielding any solutions for Flynn. Her eyes were swimming through sites on chemical compositions, processes of genetic mutation in animals, and survival of the fittest adaptations. An hour and a half and a sleeve of Oreos later, Flynn logged off feeling more hopeless than ever.

Flynn sat nervously rocking on her bed holding her converter in her shaking hands. When the call came in, she answered instantaneously, almost causing the converter to slip from her sweaty hands and fall to the floor. She recovered it, took a deep breath and then said, "Hello?"

"Flynn, is that you?"

"Yes."

"Thank Poseidon. Did you get our email?"

Again, "Yes," was all that she could manage to mutter. The talking part of the conversation this evening would belong to Caspian. So he talked and she listened, murmuring understanding as he told her their saga so he would know the connection between the converters was maintained. When he finished and paused she said,

"What are you going to do?"

"We don't know. We were hoping you could help. Any ideas? Did you look at the molecular map?"

"No, I mean, yes I looked at it, but no, I don't have any ideas. I went to the library during study hall and searched online after school and dinner, and couldn't come up with anything on the molecular structure. I'm so sorry. I do have one other idea, but it's not really worked out yet."

"Ugh. Well what good are you?" he asked in exasperation.

"Okay, genius, if things are so difficult for you, then why don't you all just come up the Tube and ask for some serious scientists to help?" Flynn asked in a childishly mocking tone.

"You really don't get it do you? You have no idea how serious this is! Flynn, listen carefully. The Tube is blocked. The Dolphins have convinced others to join their cause now. Puffer fish have somehow infiltrated the Tube and as soon as anyone initiates the process to go upward to the Surface Station, they puff up, making the trip impossible."

Silence ensued on the other end of the line.

"Flynn? Flynn!?! Are you still there?" Caspian shrieked for fear of losing their connection.

"Yeah, sorry," she said softly, "I'm here. I just can't believe it."

"I know," Caspian said, compassion and forgiveness entering his voice for the first time in the conversation. "It is just so unbelievable."

"Okay, you have my full attention now."

"Thank goodness, due time you came around. We have a plan to get the puffer fish out. But we will need your help with that."

"What about the Surface Station staff?"

"Our telecommunication lines have been sabotaged so we haven't had any contact with them. But even if we could reestablish communication, we're afraid that if they get involved, they will force us up before we can find out any information about Mom and Dad and the other missing adults."

"I totally get that. They'd want to form a committee, and have to get permission for funding the search and blah blah blah. You guys are right. And brave."

"Thanks. Any ideas?" Caspian asked.

"Well let's think this through. I'm guessing the puffer fish infiltrated the Tube from the surface, where the water feeds in to move the compartment up and down. There is no way they could break through the fiberglass wall, and they can't get in from the bottom because the only way in is through the filter system inside of the ARK. If we can get rid of the fish, then the Tube will be free for travel," she said.

"Right, but Flynn, we can't just bail ship. Mom and Dad... and the others... they're still all out there. We can't just leave them."

"I know. I know," Flynn said. "Don't worry Cas, we'll come up with something. We always do. And we'll think on it. I will call you via converter tomorrow after school. 4:00. Set your watch alarm okay?"

"Okay. Night Flynn."

"Night. And Cas, tell Noah I love you both."

"Thanks Flynn, sleep tight."

And then, the siblings disconnected their converters and both went to sleep with troubles at bay, at least for the night. Even their dreams were merciful enough to allow them some rest.

*   *   *   *   *   *   *   *   *   *

Church on Sunday morning, the week after Savannah's disappearance, ended with prayers for search efforts and for her family. It was difficult for Flynn and Nora to sit through the quiet hour, especially because they hadn't been talking that much lately. After the blow up about the email, they had been distant from each other and overwhelmed with emotions that were difficult to understand.

Here in this church, sitting in a crowded room, their eyes met and did not leave each other's face. Wordlessly they forgave each other right then and there. They were up against too much to be without each other. Psalms, songs, prayers and they found themselves holding hands part way through the service. Friends again.

Neither girl was glad for Savannah's situation. Sure they thought she was annoying and stuck up. True, they talked about her behind her back. But disliking a girl at school for petty social reasons did not mean you rejoiced in her disappearance, despite the fact that they had probably wished it in their night time conversations a dozen times in the weeks before.

Instead, Flynn and Nora brought sandwiches and

drinks down to the shoreline to feed those who were searching. They wished luck to Mr. and Mrs. Taylor and even gave them hugs. No matter how little they liked Savannah before she disappeared, they wished she'd turn up unharmed.

Chapter 40
ARK

"And whether you're on the inside or the outside, windows allow you to look past where you are."-Bryan Collier

The crew of the ARK remained diligently employed in their survival tasks, when all of a sudden, things got much worse than before. They were sitting eating a small meal and sparingly sipping their small supply of desalinified water when a large groan echoed throughout the room. The lights dimmed, and then went out. They sat in darkened silence, until the emergency lights hummed and then flickered on.

Professor Bebee's northern hardened spirit slipped from her refined mouth. "Shit." And then recovering, she sighed and dug into yet another problem full force, refusing to give up. "Alright gang, looks like we have a job to add to our list."

"Finding out how to get our power back?" asked Noah.

"No, finding out how our power source failed in the first place, and then using that information to help us return the source to our good use, and increasingly declining cause."

"Basically the same thing," said Noah.

"No," Professor Bebee said, "it is not. Finding the cause of the problem precedes finding the solution. In the most desperate of times Noah, we must use science to help us survive. Without it we have no chance."

"Right," he agreed unenthusiastically.

"This is serious. Among other things, like light and currently non-working communication systems... no power means no air filter. No air filter means no oxygen," she projected dismally. "So, anyone up for the job?" she asked.

"You know we'll always go to bat for you," Luke said

stepping up to the proverbial plate. Pac stood up too, backing up his forever best friend.

"Excellent, thank you boys. I suggest, starting in the-"

"Generator room. Got it. Thanks," And they were out the door.

After the noise of the sliding door faded, silence in the kitchen ensued. Nina broke that fragile silence like a glass dropped from clumsy fingers shattering on the floor.

"I'm sick of feeling like a fish in bowl," Nina said exasperated. "I mean, you might all be used to it, but it's different now that they are watching us. I can't handle it anymore!"

"Whoa, someone has a little aqua paranoia," Noah mumbled.

"Stop it. I don't care how ridiculous it sounds," Nina ranted and then turned to Professor Bebee.

"May I have permission to break from food collecting and water storing? We have enough to get us through the next three meals. I want to cover the observation deck window."

Skeptical, Professor Bebee turned her head as if confusion. "The entire window?" she asked.

"I have a plan, I promise you. And if I succeed, it will not only put my paranoias to rest, but also give us some more mobility around the ARK, I mean, without the fear of being seen by... by *them*," Nina said with a pleading look on her face.

"Nina, you know that every minute from here on out is precious. We are all doing our part to benefit our cause. Do you truly believe that your effort in this matter will benefit our cause? If so, then yes, you have my permission. But I want you to think carefully about this before committing your time to this task when so much else needs to be done," Professor Bebee said.

"This will help, Professor. I promise," Nina said assuredly.

"Then yes, permission granted. Good luck Nina," Professor Bebee said and then returned to her dinner, chewing thoroughly before swallowing a bony piece of fish.

Chapter 41
Surface

"I'll lean on you and you'll lean on me and we'll be okay." – Dave Matthews Band

After church, and delicious pancakes made by Mr. Nelson, the girls dashed up to their rooms, eager to show tidings of friendship, now that they were talking again.

It took thirty-five minutes to explain the entire scientific catastrophe of a situation to Nora. And when Flynn paused for a breath, with a forlorn look to Nora, Nora smiled.

"Smiling!?!?" shrieked Flynn. "I tell you about the downfall and possibly ending of my entire family and life, well prior life, and you respond by smiling!"

"Yes," was all that Nora said.

"Why?!?"

"Because now we have a project. And you know I love a good project," Nora plainly stated.

Exasperated, but relieved to have a partner in action, Flynn slumped to the bed and began to work out a masterful plan that just might be able to save her family from destruction and doom.

Yes, there is a need for the dramatics. Destruction and doom was certainly upon the remaining members of the ARK.

Nora, for her lack of scientific background, was a remarkably good planner. What practical holes her plans did have, she more than made up for in enthusiasm. The girls spent the entire afternoon in a mass planning session, breaking only for Algebra homework that was due Monday, dinner and a brain refueling snack around 9pm. They talked late into the night (nothing new for them) and came up with the following plan, enlisting their friends and local connections where needed.

The entire plan hinged on getting Flynn to the Surface Station loading dock with the necessary cargo, distracting the Surface Station scientists and staff (say that five times fast!) long enough to disembark and begin an irreversible descent in the Tube.

"Okay, so once you get to the Surface Station, and into the Tube with him, I press the red 'go' button," Nora reviewed.

"The disembarking button," Flynn corrected.

"The red one, whatever," Nora repeated while Flynn rolled her eyes.

"What if the dolphins and the other fish and what not see you coming down? Doesn't that spoil the whole point of the surprise attack?"

"Nora, we are not attacking. We are like foreign aids, like in social studies, going down to help. Remember the lecture on the United Nations last week with Mr. Dulcarney?"

"Riiiiight," Nora added unenthusiastically. "Like there is room in my brain for social studies lectures when we have all of this going on, not to mention soccer playoffs, time with Riley, SAT prep…"

"I get it, but anyway, we are not attacking, just going down to help. And we have a distraction plan."

"Right, tell me about that part again?"

"We are coinciding our descent in the Tube with something called coral spawning. Each Fall, 8 nights after the third quarter full moon, coral spawn. Or in teenager terms, send out all these little squishy balls of stuff that will make new coral. It is how the reef grows."

"And how exactly does that help us?" Nina asked, still confused.

"Well, there are so many polyps, aka: the little squishy balls that they will provide like a major distraction, like a giant beaded curtain surrounding the coral reef. A curtain to cover up our movement," Flynn explained.

"Right, I think I get it. And you know exactly when this is going to happen?"

"Yep, it happens every year, just like clockwork. The spawning lasts for about 36 hours. Hopefully that is long enough for us to complete phases one and two."

Nora, laying on her stomach on the floor, head propped up in her hands, sat up and grabbed the National Geographic monthly calendar thumb tacked to the bedroom wall. "8 days from the full moon? That's like, like two weeks from now!" she said exasperated.

"I know," said Flynn, her face falling, bummed out by the fact that her time on the surface was coming to an early and abrupt end. "But listen, the coral spawning and going down the Tube, that's the second step to the plan. There is something else we have to do first."

Before Flynn's difficult departure plan could commence, they must do something to aid those in the ARK first. In order for Flynn to descend in the Tube, the Tube must first be clear. While the fish remained in the Tube, it was impossible to use it for travel.

Noah, Luke and Pac had come up with a brilliant, albeit risky, plan to use sea snakes to attack and scare away the aforementioned puffer fish into retreat.

Flynn and Nora would need to create a diversion from the surface allowing their companions below to escape the ARK and journey to see the snakes unseen. It would be a two part plan. The email described phase one. Traveling down the tube, their own foreign aid mission, would be part two. It wouldn't solve everything, but at least it would be a good start.

They would do it on a Monday night and a Tuesday. Tuesday was a day known to Flynn to be a low key day in the Surface Station Tube departure dock. It was, however, a very busy day in the receiving dock and many people would be there unloading new equipment. Which would mean that little attention would be paid to the Tube loading dock. Scientists with new supplies are like children with new toys, they have eyes for nothing else.

Due to the precise scientific matters at hand, the plan would need to take place at a specific time. Pulling off the plan and doing so on an exact schedule would be a challenge, but it was one the girls were up for.

A Tuesday two weeks from now was circled in purple glittered ink in Flynn's assignment notebook. It would be the perfect day to skip school because the entire sophomore class had a field trip. Nora and Flynn had enlisted Riley to cover for them. This also conveniently coincided with the particular date Caspian had set for the plan to commence. Flynn and Nora would make an early appearance on the day of the field trip, making sure that an adequate number of teachers and parent chaperones saw them to make later lacks of appearance plausible. Once the field trip was underway, they would sneak away by bike to the Surface Station.

"The station is exactly 2.4 miles from the high school," Nora informed Flynn in their late night planning session. "Coach made us run there and back every Saturday morning for soccer summer training. Believe me, I know every curb and corner of that route. And we could stash our stuff in the huge Banyan tree on the corner before the station. It's far enough away from regular traffic and the actual station for us not to be seen."

"Great! Awesome. But whose bikes? We don't ride bikes to school. Your mom will know something is up if her pretty princesses want to forego their minivan chauffeured ride to school for bikes," said Flynn.

"I'll ask Danny and Kyle. They're friends of Riley's. Remember them from Savannah's party?" Nora asked with a small cringe. "Anyway, they love their bikes, but if we offer them our uneaten field trip lunches and ensure them that they're helping out a rebel cause, I'm sure they'll let us use 'em."

With the plans well-formed and their eyelids beginning to fall, the girls got ready for bed, heads swimming with the many scenarios and details that needed to go perfectly to insure their plan was a success. Maybe their biggest worry was trying to act normal. Normal meaning their giddy fashion concerned beautiful selves. To act themselves enough, so that no one, especially Mr. and Mrs. Nelson, would guess that anything out of the ordinary was in the works.

Chapter 42
ARK

"If opportunity doesn't knock, build a door." – Milton Berle

Caspian was dreaming. He was floating… in a small body of water, somewhere inside the ARK. It took him a while to figure out where he was… but then, with a bird's eye view of the observation deck, he knew.

He was not alone in the water. It was warm. It was bright. It was serene and peaceful until he felt a huge shock on his left foot, and then another zap of pain on his right elbow. The shocks and bolts of pain continued until it actually shocked him awake.

Breathing hard and rubbing his joints, he stared hard at the ceiling and listened for any noise. All was silent. He thought back on the dream he had just had. He had been floating, looking over the ARK, and there had been pain. Suddenly he realized. *I have just dreamt a solution to our broken generator! Literally, it came to me in my dreams!* He wanted to wake the others immediately and share his idea, but then he remembered their tired eyes from last night and resolved to let them sleep another half hour.

Although the memory of his dream was painful, Caspian felt better. The situation was not great, but it was looking better. He had to admit, finally talking to Flynn had something to do with it. Something about sharing the pressure of survival. That, and having more brains working on the project couldn't hurt.

Warm in his sleeping bag, clinging to two hopeful thoughts, he rolled over for another half hour of sleep himself, calculating the way his dream plan would take form in real life. It felt like he had closed his eyes for mere moments when he felt Professor Bebee gently shake him awake.

Over breakfast, Caspian told the others about his dream plan.

"We can hook up the electro-transfer cords to the jellyfish in the chandelier tank above the observation tank. Then we collect the energy given off in shocks and use it to power the generator." He looked around the table for feedback but all he heard was the chewing of the granola bars they were having for breakfast. Stillman was the first to talk.

"Well, it could work if we had more than like 100 jellyfish, instead of the three we have in the tank." Again, more chewing.

"What about this idea?" asked Anton. "We could give the three jellyfish we have, the PE328, and talk to them, explaining our situation. Then they could go out into the ocean and get more jellyfish to help us."

"Now that's a risky plan," chimed in Sonora drawing the attention of the group. "What if the jellyfish turn against us like all the other animals?"

"Not all the animals are against us. 'Cuda is on our side!" said Caspian defensively.

"Oh, I forgot, one fish in the whole ocean doesn't want to wipe out the entire human race." shot back Sonora.

"Sarcasm will not help the situation," scolded Professor Bebee. "Now, I think this is a very resourceful plan. Good thinking Caspian, using the materials accessible to solve the problem at hand. However, the plan could use some refining," she stopped to take a sip of her juice before continuing. Her well trained students waited patiently for her to continue. "Now the shock of a jellyfish emits 100 kilowatts of energy. In order to power the generator, we need 10,000 kilowatts of energy, which would mean that we would need 100 jellyfish in order to make this plan successful. I do believe that many jellyfish populate the area, but the question is, can we get them to cooperate? In regards to the PE-328, that would be an interesting experiment. We would be able to communicate our objectives to the jellyfish as well as study and monitor the changes that take place with the introduction of the chemical to the organism, all in a controlled environment," she paused, to mentally run through their options. "I think we should do it." There were nods of agreement around the table.

"Always like you to capitalize on the teachable moment Professor B." chided Pac with a smile and a soft punch to her arm. Professor Bebee nodded, with a hint of a smile hiding on her lips.

"I graciously accept your compliment Pac," Professor Bebee said nodding in his direction. "And now finally before we get down to work for the day, I believe Miss Nina has something she would like to show us."

"Right." agreed Nina. Shying away from the spotlight as usual, she quickly led them out of the kitchen. From the moment everyone left the kitchen, they were sneaking around the edge of walls, cowering in corners, basically doing everything possible to avoid being seen. Nina walked confidently in front of the group, peeking over her shoulder and struggling to hold in her giggles as she lead them toward the once wide open expanse of the observation window.

When they reached the window, Nina stood boldly in front of it, while the rest of the crew huddled behind the couches and fake shrubbery that had been the home of Nina and Caspian's nightly gatherings.

"We do not have to be afraid of being seen anymore," Nina spoke calmly, and strongly. "From now on, we can work, and eat and sleep, without being watched."

With this being said, Nina pulled a long cord, releasing rolls of fabric that cascaded down the three story window. The rolling folds of cloth fell, rippling, in sight and sound. A mix match of bed sheets, cooking aprons, tapestry curtains, pillow cases and table cloths sewn together now covered the gigantic picture window.

"Nina. This is amazing," Sonora breathed, taking in the sight.

"Dude, you rock," agreed Luke.

"How in the world did you sew these all together so fast?" Carl asked.

"Sophomore year. I have to give all the credit to my Home Economics class teacher," Nina said smiling, looking up at her handiwork. "I figured it was one less thing to worry about. And something I could do to help." Caspian found his way to her side and squeezed her hand once, and then left it there. Nina continued to stare at the now covered window, smile ever growing, nervous to look at Caspian or anyone else, afraid to end this moment too soon.

"Well, shall we get back to work?" Professor Bebee asked.

Recharged with food and a mission for the day, the eight remaining members of the ARK split up to do their delegated duties directed by their current commander: Professor Bebee.

Chapter 43
Surface

"People are people and sometimes we change our minds. But it's killing me to see you go after all this time. And we know it's never simple, never easy, never a clean break, no one here to save me."
–Taylor Swift

What a sucky birthday. What a totally sucky, soaking wet, disaster of a birthday. Flynn lay awake staring at the ceiling reflecting back on what was quite possibly the worst birthday of her life. It definitely had elements of surprise. She couldn't deny that birthday aspect was present. But the fun, happiness and hopeful feeling toward the new year... all of that was definitely missing.

There had been no presents from her parents. How could there be when they were currently missing? Not to mention the fact that the rest of her family was buried at the bottom of the ocean, facing mortal danger. No presents doesn't really compare to those worries now does it?

She felt so selfish. So her birthday wasn't perfect. Lots of kids got far less for birthdays than she did this year. And she'd been spoiled in years past, right? So maybe this was her year to get a little less. A few less presents. A little less attention. A little less happiness. So what? *Buck up,* she told herself. *Snap out of it.* But this pep talk wasn't making her feel any better. And the fact that she was still pouting made her fall into a cycle of self-loathing that did nothing to help the situation.

The only thing left to do was close her eyes, go to sleep and hope that things would look better in the morning. She did want to go to sleep, she really did, but she couldn't, not without first flashing back over the day, one last time.

Looking back, the day started out in a perfectly normal birthday fashion. She opened her eyes moments before her alarm with a giddy Christmas morning feeling inside of her. Breakfast was a crème filled Bismarck doughnut (her favorite!) with a candle in it, compliments of ma and pa Nelson. In fact, looking back, things were running smooth and clear up until lunch. That's when things started to turn.

Most high school students would not agree, but Flynn thoroughly enjoyed cafeteria food. While walking back to her table with hamburger, cheesy fries and a carton of milk balanced on her tray, she met an unfortunate fate. She didn't see the tall pink heeled shoe that stuck into the walkway. Well, she did see it, but only after she tripped and fell over it. With lunch splattered all over the floor and her fabulous birthday outfit, she glared at a pink heeled shoe could only logically belong to three people at Bay City High School. One was sitting on the floor covered in cheesy fries. The second was pulling a pickle from the hair of the first, and the third, the villain in today's story, was Savannah Taylor's best friend, the new number one mean girl in town. And the third was the only one smiling.

Incredibly, Flynn's day got worse from there. She was sitting in the driver's seat of Mr. Nelson's mini-van, asking the facilitator of the test to repeat himself.

"I'm sorry, what did you say?" Flynn asked, she was breathing deeply, through her nose, because she was afraid if she opened her mouth for even an instant longer, something inappropriate would fly out.

"I said I'm sorry Miss Brinestone. You have not passed your driver's test. Please turn off the car and take the keys out of the ignition."

"Right. That's what I thought you said."

"Look, it's really hard to parallel park a mini-van, and you can retake your test again in three weeks Miss Brinestone. Cheer up. You're not the only one who hasn't passed their road test on the first try," the facilitator said, nudging her on the arm, attempting to coax even the smallest smile out of her.

"Thank you for your time. I'll go get Mr. Nelson now." Flynn said, sliding her seat belt off and stepping out of the car. Her heart, racing only minutes ago, was now sinking. Just once, she wanted to accomplish something before Caspian. Getting her driver's license while he was stuck in the ARK had been her only plan, and now it seemed as if that once bright and shining prospect had been squashed, just like everything else had today.

"Sounds like a good plan," agreed the facilitator, following Flynn's lead out of the car.

Yeah, if you have three weeks left on the surface it sounds like a good plan. What am I supposed to do if I'm headed back to the depths of nowhere in less time than that? Some birthday. At least I still have dinner with Alex.

After what turned out to be a miserable day, she hung on to the hope of a happy ending. But as dinner started, she could see that hope was also quickly fading.

Opposed to their usual chatter, tonight as Flynn and Alex sat across from each other there was silence. The simple votive candle in the center of the table flickered and added to the romantic ambiance Flynn had only dreamed of in her previous life.

Ambiance there was, romance there was not.

"Flynn, you look beautiful tonight," Alex said and Flynn felt color rise into her cheeks. "I wanted to give you a nice night for your birthday, and that's why I'm sorry I have to tell this to you now." Flynn put down her fork and starred in to Alex's devastatingly gorgeous eyes. "Flynn, I don't think we should date anymore."

Suddenly she wasn't hungry.

Chapter 44
ARK

"Team spirit is knowing and living the belief that what a group of people can accomplish together is much larger, far greater and will exceed that which an individual can accomplish alone."
– Dianne Arias

The three jellyfish floated inside their transparent prison, their spindly appendages entwining. Slowly the chandelier began to descend in to the tank water. One would think that transporting a chandelier filled with water and live creatures from a 100 foot ceiling, through a maze of sliding doors, to a low level tank would be the difficult part of the maneuver, but no, the truly challenging part still remained to be done.

The submerged chandelier hung suspended in the middle of the tank. Stillman, fully clad in wet suit and using the only remaining SCUBA tank, was anxiously waiting for it. He looked up to get the thumbs up sign from Luke above, telling him they were ready for him to release the jellyfish.

Now, you may or may not know, but jellyfish can be extremely dangerous to humans and other sea creatures. A single jolt or sting from a tentacle can render the receiver paralyzed, thus the tense feeling that permeated the space as Stillman cautiously approached the chandelier.

Pac and Carl waited above to pull him out, as soon as the Jellyfish were released. Sonora and Nina stood on the opposite side of the tank, ready to distract the jellyfish with flashlights and laser pointers, should they decide to attack Stillman. He took as deep a breath as possible with a SCUBA mask attached to his face and extended his gloved hand to the chandelier. He counted to himself, one, two, three, and then…

flipped the release switch.

Instantly he was swimming up and out of the tank, readily looking for his escape. Pac and Carl had him up and out in no time, but when Stillman looked down at the chandelier, nothing had changed. The jellyfish were staying inside the chandelier, even though the door hung wide open. Relief swept though everyone. Nina wondered if they whole charade of the exit plan and distractions were necessary, but soon she would realize what all the fuss was about.

"They aren't moving. Do you think they are stunned from the move from the ceiling to the tank?" Carl asked.

"Well, maybe, but maybe they are just getting used to their new surroundings… Let's wait and see…" Sonora explained.

Sure enough, given time to feel unthreatened, tentacles began emerging from the chandelier to test the water, and sense the level of safety. Slowly, inch by inch, the jellyfish began to exit the chandelier. As soon as they had fully abandoned the light cavity, Caspian and Luke pulled the chandelier out of the water and prepared the electro receptors for entry into the tank. Within a few minutes the transition was made. The chandelier was removed and the energy collector receptors were underwater.

Dangling motionless in the water, the jellyfish floated warily on all sides of the receptors, not sure what to make of them. Suddenly they lashed out, striking the receptors with their tentacles transferring their energy to the receptors. The control screen was a flurry of lighted panels, a computer visual of the amount of collected energy.

"I thought you said they shocked people. I see the receiver going crazy… the energy spiking on the screen… but, I don't see… I mean, in the water… nothing changes." Nina floundered verbally, as she tried to organize her thoughts out loud.

"The shock cannot be seen like, let us say, lightning.

But trust me, the effect is nearly as strong and detrimental to your body," Professor Bebee explained.

"Oh. Right," Nina said, feigning understanding. *How can something so powerful be unseen?*

"Alright gang, now that some of our needed energy is collected, let's move on to phase two of this experiment. Anton, do you have the PE-328?"

"Yes ma'am, I do," Anton said stepping forward.

"Please, for lack of a better and more scientific term, dump," and she stopped to let the giggles pass. "Yes, I said dump. Please Mr. Anton, dump the vile of PE-328 into the tank."

Unceremoniously, Anton bent over the tank, and dumped the solution into the water. Its green color stayed pooled near the top of the tank, before slowly filtering down through the layers of the water. Many seconds later the potion visibly reached the jellyfish. Sonora gasped audibly as the potion touched the outstretched tentacles of the jellyfish.

"Sorry, I guess I'm a little excited. I mean, you know we started this thing like three years ago, and now… now we are going to see how it works. I'm excited. Excited, that's all," Sonora explained with color rising in her cheeks. Nina, standing next to her, gave her shoulders a quick squeeze, partially because she was excited too, and partially because she was happy to see someone else unable to completely keep their emotions in check.

Everyone turned their attention back to the tank and focused on the living beings inside, waiting for the change. They knew it probably wouldn't be a visible change, but strained their eyes anyway, wanting so badly to see the beginning signs of change that had completely turned their world inside out.

Minutes passed, but only minutes, before a voice emerged from the mass of tangled flesh that was tentacles, "What are you staring at?"

"Holy-"

"Professor, there has been enough swearing out of you for one day," Caspian warned, never far from his professional scientific brain. "Just watch."

"Well somebody better say something," Stillman hissed through his teeth.

"Dude. What's up?" Pac asked waving toward the tank.

"Nice. Real professional," Caspian scolded.

"Lay off man, they've been able to talk for like 4 seconds. I'm sure their higher order levels of thinking aren't fully installed yet," Luke defended his best friend.

"Right, well, we should try asking them a question," Nina suggested

"Is anyone taking notes?" Professor Bebee asked

"Hello?" a voice from within the tank called "Anyone out there willing to take a chill pill to tell us what's going on?"

"See, they do speak teen," Pac gloated. Caspian uncharacteristically rolled his eyes as Pac continued to explain, "Here's the deal jelly-dudes. We are scientists, I know, we look young, our parents are the real deal, we're just fakin' it til we make it right now. But anyway, we all worked together to create this solution that was supposed to eat away pollution in the ocean. Bummer is, it actually gave you, meaning every living creature underwater, human intelligence, maybe other super powers too, but we haven't got it totally figured out yet. So, basically you can speak and think like humans."

"Wicked," the jellyfish taking the lead said.

"Agreed," Luke nodded. "Now that that is out of the way, we have to get down to business. Got names or want us to give them to you?"

"What do we look like? Your pets?" the jellyfish shot back

"Sorry, no offense meant," Pac sheepishly apologized.

"Some taken, but forgiven. I'm Jett, and these are my parents, Adriel and Steve."

"I told you he was a teen," Pac said glaring at Carl.

"Right, now that business you were talking about?" Jett asked.

"So, you're in then? You don't hardcore hate us for… for… for changing you?" Luke tentatively asked.

"Dude, I live in a chandelier with negative personal space. With my parents. Wouldn't you be ready for a change?"

"Right. Okay, business it is," Pac continued to be the lead speaker for the group, seeing as how he and Jett spoke the same language. "See the other sea creatures, they aren't quite as cool with the whole transformation. I mean, they like the change, they just decided to abuse the privilege and now they kind of want to take over the world."

"A bit dramatic, even for a teenager, don't you think?" asked Jett.

"Not really," Luke added. "They told us all this themselves. They're pissed because humans screwed up their whole eco-system and now they want revenge. Dramatic doesn't actually cover it."

"Cool. I mean, not cool, but count us in," Jett nonchalantly committed.

**Chapter 45
Surface**

*"When I wake up in the morning is it gonna be another ugly day?"
– Something Corporate*

Waking up after a hard day is almost worse than actually living the day. Because you wonder if that day, the day you are on the threshold of, is going to be another horrible day, or if this one, this new day, will find a way to grant you some mercy and allow you to float invisibly through it.

Invisibility might be too much to ask. I did just get dumped by the hottest guy in school. All the girls will undoubtedly be floating with glee, and snuggling up to Alex any chance they get. And I am going to have to watch it all, and listen to them whisper behind my back as I walk down the hall. At least Savannah won't be there to join that party. That was mean. Ugh, maybe I deserve this. Maybe this is karma for wanting too much, and for taking it all without thinking when it fell into my lap. Thank Poseidon it is Friday and it will be just one more day until the weekend. Hopefully someone else will do something excitingly awful over the weekend and by Monday, my misery will no longer be center stage. Geez, am I immune from even one second of self-centered thought? Guess not. Might as well get out of bed and face my punishment. Guess I deserve it.

"Hey there sunshine," Nora said, sticking her head in the door, already out of the shower, towel around her head, dressed in jeans and a sequined ribbed tank.

"Sunshine and daisies. That's me," mumbled Flynn, pulling her legs from under the covers.

"No, don't get up quite yet. I have something for you," Nora said, coming in to lay on top of the covers next to Flynn. She pulled a wrapped present from behind her back. Pink paper and ribbons. "I didn't have a chance to give this to you yesterday. Happy Birthday. Belated, of course. But we know that something stylish always arrives fashionably late."

"Thanks Nora," Flynn said, smiling, and infinitely grateful for her best friend. Flynn unwrapped a tan colored book, with multicolored leaves, wrapping their way around the cover. A red elastic strap stretched across the front of the book, holding its covers closed, keeping the owner's secrets safely tucked inside.

"It's a journal. I thought you might want to write down your thoughts. Since you have so many of them. I thought you might want to remember your time up here," Nora explained.

"You mean remember being dumped?" Flynn choked out, a single tear sliding down her face.

"Aww hunnie. Really?" Nora asked wiping the tear away.

"Yeah. He said he saw us more as friends. What a great memory. I'm sure I'll want to remember every unbearable moment of that dinner," Flynn spit out. Then took a deep breath and said, "But thank you, this is a great gift. I will fill it with memories of you. And pictures of sunsets on the beach, and movie tickets and all sorts of surface stuff. Too bad I can't capture the smell of beach bonfire in a journal," Flynn added, starting to feel better. Maybe today wouldn't be so bad.

"You are welcome. Now let's get out of bed and get you looking fabulous. There's no way anyone will be saying anything bad about my girl today," Nora said pulling Flynn out of bed. "And let's put that birthday cash to good use today after school. The mall should have their new season lines out by now. There's plenty of damage to be done there."

Flynn turned to look across the room at her amazing friend, "Nora, have you ever considered a career in psychology?"

"Not really, why?"

"Because you put a Percocet to shame. Seriously Nora,

you are better than a pharmaceutical wonder. At least for me," Flynn raved. "Thank you."

"No worries chica. Now get dressed," Nora demanded. "Breakfast in ten."

Worries subsided, Flynn did as she was told, then grabbed her bag and added her new journal to her regular load of books. Flynn's meticulous and scientific upbringing should have made her a prime candidate for journaling. Not to mention all the field research and data computer systems she had experience with – in all their record keeping glory. No, the Type A personality urge of logging her daily thoughts in an organizational manner had previously eluded her. Until now. Alex breaking up with her, despite the reason, woke her up to the fact that she couldn't take her time on the surface or the things she witnessed here for granted.

She made a resolution to catalog her favorite things on the surface so she could visit them later, in the (via the eyes of Flynn) cold coffin of the ARK. One step better than recording her adventures, sights, sounds, and somehow smells, Flynn decided to make a list, a checklist of things she wanted to see and accomplish in her remaining days on land.

Bounding down the stairs with a new sense of purpose, she bounced into the kitchen ready to share her plan with her reliable sidekick.

"Hey Nora, wanna work on a project?" Flynn asked, eyebrows raised in excited anticipation.

"You know projects are my favorite," Nora answered enthusiastically through a mouthful of cereal.

"Finish your breakfast, and meet me on the front porch. I'll fill you in while we wait for your dad to be ready to go. I'm doing breakfast on the go, granola bar. See you out there."

Spurred by curiosity, Nora inhaled the rest of her breakfast and then raced in her pink flip flops throughout the house to get her school stuff together. She met Flynn on the steps moments later to find her sketching the Nelson's front yard and mailbox.

"I gave you that so you could record your favorite moments and memories of your time on the surface, and you choose to draw my mailbox?" Nora asked, sitting down on the step next to Flynn.

"Did somebody sprinkle a little sass instead of sugar on their cereal this morning?" Flynn teasingly poked back.

"You guessed it. Gotta add some spice to life every once and a while." Nora smiling sweetly replied, "Now what's this brilliant project you had in mind?"

Flynn described for Nora her list idea and by the time the backseat ride to the high school ended, the list included 14 must accomplish items ranging from all night *L.A. Living* marathon to visiting Disney World, from getting mani-pedis to making a video of all of Flynn's favorite surface people. Project in mind, journal in hand and best friend in stride, Flynn faced the new day. Her days on the surface were numbered and she was determined to make them count.

Chapter 46
ARK

"Call it a clan, call it a network, call it a tribe, call it a family. Whatever you call it, whoever you are, you need it." – Jane Howard

They continued to collect energy from Jett and his parents throughout the day, talking as they went. Strangely, teenage jellyfish and teenage humans were not all that different. It seems that parental confinement, forced expectations and emotional rollercoasters translated, no matter how your DNA was constructed. Pac especially connected with Jett, and had taught him all about Obscoral, pointing out different features of the tank and the way they contributed to the game. Jett had seen them playing it, hanging from his ceiling vantage point and was totally pumped to be clued in on all the rules. They worked on somehow safely involving him, the key being safely. Jett thought he could be some sort of additional obstacle, like a traveling goalie of sorts. But Pac pointed out that if he turned out to be good at his role in the game, the rest of the boys may be too paralyzed to play anymore… or talk… or blink. So there were some wrinkles to iron out. It was nice to have another animal on their side though. Maybe this whole thing wasn't going to end so badly after all.

With the current success of the jellyfish transformation and the power to the generator restored, their confidence began to grow. Heading to the League of the Dark Vines was looking more like a practical plan than a suicide mission.

After an emotionally draining day, the crew bedded down in their sleeping bags to talk through tomorrow's plan one last time.

"Tell me again why they call it the League of the Dark Vines?" Nina asked.

"It's like a forest of vines, growing down from the surface. It's really dark and super dangerous," Sonora explained between yawns. "Even if the grown-ups were here, Carl's the best pilot we've got. He practically grew up in the cockpit of the SQUID."

"The SQUID?"

"It's a hybrid-vehicle. Part robot, part submarine. Super complicated to maneuver, but like I said, Carl's the best."

Nina glanced nervously at Carl and then tentatively asked, "What do you think Carl?"

"Well, it won't be easy, but I think we can do it."

"We? Who's traveling with you?" Nina asked.

"Caspian. He insisted."

Nina's heart sank to her stomach.

"Oh," Nina choked out. "No one told me."

Caspian walked into the kitchen, finishing a conversation with Anton. Nina's eyes darted to his face, locked eyes for a brief moment and then immediately dropped them to her hands that sat wringing in her lap.

"So... ah yeah. All gassed up and ready to go." Caspian continued hesitantly. "Carl, the GPS all ready to go?"

"Yep, and I oiled the arms and checked the pressuring mechanism for the cockpit too."

"Perfect. I guess we're all set for tomorrow then," Caspian concluded.

"It will be worth it you guys," encouraged Anton.

"Easy for you to say Anton, you aren't going," challenged Carl.

"If there was another seat, I'd-"

"Oh don't start! Convenient there are only 2 seats," Carl shot back.

"Fine!" Anton shouted. "You stay, I'll go!"

"Enough!" Nina pleaded. And when she spoke, the

small room became silent. "Please," she said quietly. "Please. This is your home. I have been here far shorter a time than any of you, and I want to fight tooth and nail for this place. We need to do what we need to do. And right now, that means, getting Carl and Caspian and the SQUID ready to travel to the League of the Dark Vines tomorrow. It means convincing the sea snakes to join our side and stand against the dolphins and finish this thing." Everyone was quiet for a long long time before Nina spoke again. "We can't do this without the sea snakes, but we definitely can't do it without each other."

"Well said, Miss Nelson," affirmed Professor Bebee. "Well said. Now the last thing we need to prepare before their journey tomorrow is alert Flynn the mission is a go."

"I can go email her before I go to sleep, Professor," said Luke.

"Thank you Luke. I would appreciate that. Now, all that being said, let's all turn in for the night. Get as much sleep as we can before another big day tomorrow." Then, she blew out the candle nearest her, and slid down into her sleeping bag, punched her pillow twice and laid her head down.

With one last audible sigh, Nina caught Caspian's eye, gave a weak smile and then rolled over and gave into sleep.

Chapter 47
Surface

"Success can be found in much smaller portions than people realize. At times we live our life on a paper thin edge that barely separates mediocrity and success from failure."
– Michael Johnson (Olympic Sprinter)

If anyone asked, they were at the 8:45 showing of the latest romantic comedy at the Mega Plex 16. But anyone who knows a sixteen year old girl who recently broke up with her boyfriend, knows she would never go see a romantic comedy so soon. No, the dynamic duo of Flynn and Nora had a different destination on this particular night. Riley could barely see their struggling forms across the water as he sat and watched from his car on the pier.

Flynn's hair was strewn across her face as the wind whipped wickedly past her. She struggled with the weather worn oars with each labored stroke. *Just a little bit further*, she thought, *just a little more*. She knew if she looked up she would see Nora huddled at the back end of the row boat clinging desperately to side of the boat for balance and also to the several buckets carefully placed at her feet, attempting to keep them from spilling. *This has to work, it just has to. I don't know what we'll do if it doesn't. For the love of Poseidon, please work!*

"I see it! Flynn, we're there!" Nora exclaimed pointing to a place behind Flynn's mane of wild blonde hair. Flynn turned to look, holding strong to the oars, afraid the waves would pull them from her. Nora was right. She could see it just ahead. The Mausoleum.

It had been an old factory, a button factory to be exact. A pompous, old, and very stubborn Spaniard had built the factory on the coastline almost one hundred years before. He built the foundation of his button dreams right on the coast, so as to avoid payment for shipping of the shells used to make his treasured buttons. Flynn's grandfather had told the Brinestone children stories of his father collecting shells, searching the beach and shallow waters, finding buckets of them, and turning them into the stingy man for extra money.

When Hurricane Gloria came in 1935, his stubborn streak showed its true colors when he refused to leave. The wind and the waves came, and the button maker would not go. Eventually, the wind and waves took the button maker for themselves. And with it, they took the factory too.

Now, here it lay, half sunken in the coastal waters of Bay City, Florida. It has become home to the locals and tourists alike, known as the best of the best for fishing, snorkeling, swimming and scuba diving. But more importantly, it had also become home for the coral. The button factory, so full of tiny shell buttons, was now covered in coral that used its framework as the foundation for their reef. The reef began at the Mausoleum and grew for miles in one direction out to sea. The coral was their true destination on this stormy night.

As Flynn held their position, Nora clambered to stand and dump pail after pail of neon bits of metal and rubber into the turbulent water. When she was finished, Flynn maneuvered the row boat one hundred and eighty degrees and started back toward the shore. As they traveled, the wind too loud to allow them to talk, the girls silently wished with all their hearts. Wished and hoped that their plan would work.

While Flynn's arms worked vigorously, her brain was busy too. She remembered the day when coral spawning had first been explained to her. She couldn't believe she hadn't heard about this marine phenomenon before her surface school experience. She had been at school, the surface school, in science. Mr. Bottleberke had begun a lecture on asexual reproduction. Aside from her dislike of water, she actually thought that the life found within it was absolutely fascinating. Mr. Bottleberke had told them that every year, on the 8th day after the third quarter full moon, the coral would spawn. *Spawn. What a weird word. It sounds like something utterly disgusting that lives in one of Noah's comic books.* But in fact, spawning had turned out to be the answer to her problem.

Flynn had shared the basic concept of her plan with Caspian and the others via email. It was a convenient way to communicate, considering their distance, and Flynn's busy daily schedule. In Flynn's email, she asked for them to gather what information they could about coral spawning, think about her plan and to respond by 4:00 the following day. Caspian, with the help of Professor Bebee was able to follow through on her requests and the following email was in Flynn's email inbox as instructed and on time.

  Flynn,
  Hey, genius idea. I have full confidence of its success. The timing is perfection. Pending each of our individual roles, we should be able to make it work.
  Carl and I are going to use the chaotic activity of the spawning as a curtain of distraction to travel to the League of the Dark Vines. Communication with the sea snakes is imperative if we hope to rid the Tube of the puffer fish. Professor Bebee is unsure that the coral spawning on its own will be enough to distract the creatures of the sea to the point that they would not notice the SQUID traveling away from the ARK. We need to add another element of surprise to occupy the attention of those watching over the ARK.
  This is where you and Nora come into play. At the designated time, the two of you will load a large supply of brightly colored lures, jigs and sinkers (you know, surface fishing equipment) into a row boat and travel out to the Mausoleum (Nina told us that Nora would know where this is).
  At 9:00pm exactly, dump the supply of fishing gear overboard. The thought is that the brightly colored bits of plastic fishing equipment, along with the millions of coral

polyps floating through the water, would cloud the vision of the guards and allow the SQUID to travel away unnoticed. Professor Bebee also suspected that the guarding fish spend so much time on watch that they had little time to hunt for themselves. Seeing what they think to be a buffet line of food, she hopes they will leave their posts in order to grab a quick bite to eat. At least, this is the plan.

Let us know what you think, and if you will be able to fulfill your part of the plan. Flynn, we need you more than you know. More than ever now. Be in touch soon.

~ Caspian

After reading the email through twice she thought, *it just has to... It just has to work.*

"You know I will have to tell my parents something when Nina doesn't come back," Nora mentioned on their way home, hands held to the heat vents in Riley's car.

"We could say that she is participating in an extended field experience seminar," Flynn suggested from the back seat.

"We could fake the permission slips, get Simon to deliver them," Nora continued.

It was both comfortable and scary the way they could finish each other's thoughts and sentences. It was almost as if they could have an entire conversation without saying a word at all.

Flynn knew this would be one of the things she would miss the most, spending time with the one person who understood her better than anyone else. Everyone in the ARK needed endless explanations to her seemingly foreign actions, and it annoyed her, it made her feel more lonely than anything. *How can I be so different than you, that you need me to explain this? Don't any of you understand?* She had had that thought countless times in the previous years of her life. She fought hard to forget it, because acknowledging it would make going back down even more unbearable than it already was.

Chapter 48
ARK

"No other road. No other way. No day but today." – RENT

They sat in the SQUID docking station waiting for the early signs that the spawning had begun. Sure enough, small M&M sized organisms started to pass by the window. Over the next half hour they increased in number until a colorful blizzard swirled around the ARK.

Nina, originally being from Wisconsin, reminisced about her childhood winters in waist deep snow. Noah especially enjoyed hearing of this magical snow that could be transformed into tall round men, domed shaped houses and lakes of sheer ice. For a brief moment he understood Flynn's desire to discover the joys and excitements of the surface.

They had sent 'Cuda ahead, to wake and warn the sea snakes of their arrival and let them know that this was a peaceful mission and not an attack. Being one of the few undecided creatures left in the ocean, the snakes were on the defensive. No need to alarm them and risk losing their help, before they even had a chance to share their plan.

'Cuda left his secret hold, the underside of an abandoned loading dock deck tunnel, thirty minutes before Carl and Caspian were to load the SQUID. He swam in a direct route to the Kelp Forest, navigating through the dangerous terrain of sleeping enemies. *This better work, or I'm as good as fish food.*

Strange as it was, Caspian was having that same thought as he crawled into the SQUID next to Carl. After they were both in position, Luke handed down the emergency survival kit of hand held compressed oxygen tanks, goggles, nutrition bars and a CD full of good pump up tunes to get them psyched for their task ahead. Caspian raised his eyebrows at the last item in the pack and Luke said, "Hey, you never know man. Surface scientists have done loads of studies on the power of keeping a positive mind set. What's not positive about a little music runnin' through your brain?"

With a shrug, Caspian stowed the pack beneath his seat, and for Luke's benefit, slid the homemade compilation mix into the CD player on the SQUID dashboard. With one more look upward through the roof window, and a wave to the now remaining commanding crew of the ARK, they were off.

Carl nudged the SQUID out of the docking station slowly, like a car at a stop sign, checking to see if the coast was clear. He couldn't see any guards, but then again, he couldn't see much, except the coral polyps and colored fishing gear dropped by the girls above. Combined, there must have been millions.

"Flynn must have held off from buying shoes from the surface stores for the last few months to be able to afford all of these… these…" Caspian struggled to come up with an adequate name and settled for, "these tiny wiggly things."

Carl, relieved for the break of tension, let out one burst of a laugh and then began to travel away from the ARK and toward the League of the Dark Vines. Although seeing was difficult, they trusted the route provided by the GPS and continued toward their destination with increasing speed.

All they could do now was sit back, watch and wait.

Chapter 49
ARK

"I apologize to big questions for small answers."
– Wislawa Szybroska

    They had been gathering all morning, ever since Caspian and Carl had left under the cloak of beautiful distraction. Creatures of the deep, coming out of hiding, coming together, united in force against the humans. At least, in this their first attack, against the humans they knew best and had access to: the humans in the ARK.

    Professor Bebee, Nina, Sonora, Stillman, Nora, Luke, Pac and Anton stood openly on the observation deck watching the crowd culminate in front of them. For a short time, curiosity and wonder took the place of fear. What were these animals planning to do?

    It was clear that they could communicate, although those inside the ARK could not hear their voices. The animals were organized in row-like lines ascending from the ocean floor, towering up above the top surface of the ARK. Watching from the observation deck, their eyes were drawn to the far left end where a column of dolphins raised a single pectoral fin, to which the army of fish turned to face right as a single unit. Now they were lined tail to snout. Then, they began to swim. Around the ARK they went. Again and again and again. The dolphins and the swordfish and the tuna and the threadfin and all the others had been swimming in a continuous direction for over an hour, when curiosity was quickly replaced by understanding. The animals were trying to create a whirlpool, with the ARK at its center, making it vulnerable to the immense gravitational pull of the whirlpool. Trying and succeeding.

"What do we do?" gasped Sonora. "I mean, what can we do?"

"We have no need to fear for our immediate safety," Professor Bebee spoke in a tense calm. "The central unit of the ARK can withstand the immense pressure of the water that surrounds it. Even if they can create a whirlpool large enough to remove the water around us, the pressure of the water will be replaced gradually by the gravitational pull of the pool." A visible sigh of relief escaped from all those standing on the observational deck. "It's the outer branches of the ARK that we need to be concerned about."

"The garden…"

"The computer wing…"

"The water garage, our WakeTecs…"

"Geez Noah, way to be serious," chided Sonora.

"I am being serious, how are we going to get around?"

"Oh my god! Caspian! And Carl!" Nina cried. "How are they going to get back?!?!"

A deadly silence, gripped the crew of the ARK.

Chapter 50
Surface

"Nothing is perfect. Life is messy Relationships are complex. Outcomes are uncertain." – Hugh Mackay

There is nothing I can do right now to help. Literally nothing, Flynn thought as the Nelson family minivan cruised down the highway closer to the happiest place on Earth.

Today was the day of their Disney World adventure. Flynn feeling childish excitement, literally bounced in the backseat. She was determined to enjoy today despite her sleep deprivation from last night's escapades as well as her family's impending doom.

"Can we get two of those hats? You know the ones with the ears?" she asked mimicking the round mouse ears with her fists on top of her head.

"Anything you want," Nora appeased.

"And Splash Mountain?"

"Splash Mountain and Space Mountain as many times as you want."

"Have I told you guys you are the best?" Flynn asked leaning toward the front seats.

"Only about a thousand times since you arrived, and another solid hundred this morning," Mrs. Nelson laughed. "But you are entirely welcome dear. We're just glad that you have enjoyed your stay so much. It's sad to think that it is almost over."

"I know. But hey, maybe my parents loved Nina so much they won't want to send her back," Flynn half joked.

"You know we love you hun, but we'll be glad to get Nina back. You never know, maybe you'll be back here sooner than you think," Mr. Nelson added. "I can't imagine Nora without you. You two are like twins separated at birth that have finally found each other."

"Totally," Nora chimed in avoiding the Nina subject as much as possible. "You sure we just can't adopt her?"

"Nora, she's not a puppy," Mr. Nelson chided.

"You're right, I'm way cuter!" Flynn said. "I shed, but I don't drool!" They laughed the day away and enjoyed some of Flynn's final hours on the surface soaking in the sun and fun.

Hours later, after the Haunted Mansion, Tea Cups, Pirates of the Caribbean, a picture in front of Cinderella's castle, the Rockin' Rollercoaster, the Tower of Terror, Alien Encounter, endless rides on both Splash Mountain and Space Mountain and the Epcot fireworks show, Flynn and Nora collapsed in the backseat Mickey hats tipped low over their eyes, dreaming of their perfect last weekend together.

Chapter 51
ARK

"Fear? What should a man fear? It's all chance, chance rules our lives. Not a man on Earth can see a day ahead, groping through the dark. Better to live at random, best we can." – Sophocles (The Oedipus Plays)

The vines came into view about forty minutes after their departure. The boys sat up from their relaxed position and began preparing for arrival.

"Are you sure you know what you are going to say?" asked Carl.

"Yes," Caspian answered resolutely.

"Do you want to go over it one more time?"

"What? The twenty seven times we went over it yesterday, and the four more times just now weren't enough?" asked Caspian exasperated.

"Well, I guess they were," conceded Carl. "I just know how perfectly exact you like things, and I guess I was just trying to be helpful."

"Geez, maybe Flynn has been right all these years. Maybe I do need to relax a little bit. Is that the way everyone thinks of me?"

"Honestly?"

"Honestly."

"Well, yes. Most people see you as a little up-tight, uber-scientific, overly analytic and ah…"

"Really, that's enough."

"Right."

"Carl?"

"Yes?"

"Thank you. For being honest. That takes a real friend."

"No problem," Carl said with a wide smile, relieved that Caspian wasn't mad, or worse, hurt by his quick appraisal. "Hey," he said, attempting to change the subject, "Wanna go hang out with some sea snakes, try not to get eaten, and while we're at it, attempt to save our family and friends?"

"Why not add saving the world to our to do list?" joked Caspian.

"Sure," laughed Carl. "If there's time."

A tap on the window brought them back to the task and danger at hand. It was 'Cuda. Seriousness took the front seat again.

"They know you are coming. They are open to communicating with you." Even though Caspian had talked to 'Cuda dozens of times before this encounter, it was always so strange to see his fish lips moving and to simultaneously hear human words coming out of his mouth.

"Thanks 'Cuda," nodded Caspian.

"How do we proceed?" asked Carl, hands on the steering wheel.

"I'll go first, keep your headlights on me. I'll lead you to them. They've taken to residing deep in their vines," said "Cuda, turning to go.

Carl and Caspian, in the SQUID, followed 'Cuda's blue-green swishing tail through the dark vines for nearly thirty minutes. Slowly the vines began to become sparse, and they found themselves in a clearing, alone. 'Cuda nodded and Carl and Caspian suited up into SCUBA tanks (one more having been found inside of the SQUID while checking it earlier for equipment), facemasks and wet suits, and exited the SQUID. Still it was just the three of them in the clearing. As they swam to meet 'Cuda in the center of the clearing, Carl asked, "'Cuda, where are the sea snakes?" 'Cuda silently used his fin to point upward.

The sea snakes descended from the vines that

surrounded the clearing and the SQUID. Chills raced up Caspian's spine that had nothing to do with the water temperature. He tried to restore pace to his galloping heart rate as he switched on the microphone and intercom on his helmet. Then he took a deep breath, preparing to speak to the nest of snakes. As he did this, one snake slithered forward, separating itself from the rest. It was there that Caspian directed his voice when he said, "We mean you no harm. We are here beca-"

"We know why you ssseek us," the snake interrupted. "You may call me Pelamis. We wish to ssspeak directly to the barracuda. We feel this will make our encounter more natural and that is what we desssire." Caspian agreed with his statement and nodded to 'Cuda, who now assumed the role of chief communicator.

"Even in this new altered world order, we find ourselves at the bottom of the food chain, in fact, ssseizing lesss power than before. We do not wisssh to be all powerful and mighty as sssome do. We would rather give up thisss gift of ssspeech and return to our more independent and ssseculded livesss." Pelamis spoke, and then continued, "We wisssh to aide you in your endeavorsss againssst the Fishssspeakers, if you sssubmit to our our conditionsss. What ssay you and your companionsss barracuda?"

Nodding to 'Cuda, Caspian urged them on.

"They are eager to listen to your conditions Pelamis," 'Cuda said.

"We offer our ssservices in return for sssafe passage to and from our sssacred vinesss, and alssso that once regularity isss ressstored to the watersss, you will leave usss in peace."

Again, nodding his message of consent, Caspian looked encouragingly at 'Cuda.

"It is agreed," 'Cuda said to the snakes. "When would you wish to leave?"

"As sssoon as possible Baracuda. The fassster things

resssume to normalcy, the better it would be for our clan of sssea sssnakes. The interrogationsss and the hiding in our vinesss from the Fishssspeakers is quite exhausssting. We sssimply wisssh to live in sssolitude."

"Good. We will wait for your signal that the nest is ready to leave," 'Cuda communicated, and then turned toward the boys. He was met by a swift current of water in the face. "I hadn't noticed before, during the negotiations, but the current is building. That is very odd, for this time of year, and these parts."

"I agree," said Carl, "but we can't look alarmed. Stillman told me if we panic, the sea snakes will do the same."

Soon the current was so torrent that the boys agreed they needed to return to the SQUID.

"Carl, go ahead and prepare the SQUID for departure. I will relay our message of hastened departure to 'Cuda and Pelamis."

"Got it. But hurry. I have a bad feeling about this," Carl said, beginning to swim backwards in the direction of the awaiting doors of the SQUID.

"Agreed. See you there," Caspian said and turned his back on Carl in order to talk to 'Cuda. "'Cuda, this current is getting out of control. Would you please tell Pelamis we will wait until they are ready to leave, but will be aboard the SQUID until that time arrives?"

"I think that sounds like a good plan. I will tell them."

It was slow going as Caspian struggled to get back to the SQUID. The vines were whipping across his face, and if not for his facemask, he would have surely lost an eye. For a fearful moment he actually thought he was moving backward. And then the moment spanned into two. Yes he was definitely moving backward. He could see Carl's panic stricken face in the cockpit of the SQUID. Carl cried out, helpless to aid Caspian. Caspian powerfully kicked his flipper clad feet and stretched a hand forward, desperately trying to reach the open door of the SQUID.

In the blink of his goggled eyes, Caspian's hopes of safety were washed away, along with the SQUID. He tumbled head over heels, thrashing in the current unaware of his direction of travel or surroundings. Occasionally he caught sight of a fish tail, but mostly vines and the swirl of the tide cluttered his vision.

One minute he was in the League of the Dark Vines and the next he was out, clear of the Kelp Forest. A rock jutted up from the ocean floor and passed through Caspian's field of vision. He knew he was half as likely to crash into it as he was to grab hold of the stalagmite-like rock. Still no other options were presenting themselves at the moment. The rock was drawing nearer. Closer, closer, closer, wham. Caspian slammed into the rock.

Chapter 52
Surface

"Sometimes the hardest thing and the right thing are the same."
– The Fray

Flynn sat at the public beach nearest to the Nelson home with her now trusty running companion, Luke, sitting by her side. She paged through her journal, reviewing her recorded thoughts, double checking to make sure she hadn't missed a single moment, a single second of this sun filled surface life that she knew she would miss desperately.

Nora, as always, knew exactly where to find her. She took up her customary position and sat next to Flynn in the sand. Shifting their feet in silence for minute, feeling the sand slide between their toes, neither knew just what to say. Words seemed so small in a moment this big. How do you say goodbye to a best friend you have just found? How can you walk away from something so good when it hurts so bad? How? You walk away because you have a responsibility bigger than your feelings, bigger than yourself. Flynn knew what she needed to do. She just really really really did not want to do it.

"How's that list comin'?" Nora managed to ask.

"Decent. Just a few things left. Eat an entire ice cream cone in the sun before it melts. Bag up some beach sand near the bonfire pit. Take one last picture with you," Flynn answered softly, barely choking out the last item on her list.

"We've got a few hours left right? We can make it. I mean, make the best of it. Plenty of time to bawl our eyes out later right?"

"Right... just give me five more minutes here."

Five minutes turned into ten, turned into fifteen. The two friends sat side by side, holding hands, staring into the sun, trying hard not to think about anything past this moment. Remembering the greatest memories of a short lived friendship the way an artist compiles songs for their greatest hits CD, the girls scrolled through the highs in their few months together. Surface or ocean, above or below, next to each other or across the distances, together they had learned one of life's most important lessons: What you do in life matters far less than who you share it with.

Chapter 53
Unknown Ocean Waters

"With the dawn there comes a brand new start, another day is born, life's just begun. Hold on. Hold on. Don't give up!" – lyrics from Hold On

He hung on. He hung on. He hung on. And for what seemed like an eternity, that was all he could do, hang on.

After what seemed like ages, he chanced a look up, which meant forward. Forward into a swirling current of water that was making its way around his twig of a body in the torrent current. The vortex was growing larger, its powerful control spinning out further and further across the ocean floor. Quickly, his head snapped back down. The force of the water was too much. He feared the strain on his neck muscles would snap his head clean off.

Hang on, he thought, *just hang on.* For a while it was the only thing he could manage to waste energy on. *Hang on. Just hang on.* And then, there comes that point, the point in time when your body knows, that the end is near, that there isn't much time left. And your body allows your brain to wander. Your body allows your brain a bit of time to reflect and look back, because somehow it knows that a few moments of clarity, sanity, and tranquility are a small gift that it can give you in your last minutes.

It was as Caspian began to slip into this hypnotic daze when he began to focus on something. Well actually his eyes began to focus on this unknown object without full cooperation of his brain. Caspian had gotten as far into his self-preservation spell to see a vision of his tenth birthday. He was remembering his very first WakeTec and how he thought it was the most amazing present ever. It seem so real. Like it was floating right before his eyes. And then, he blinked. And he blinked again. It wasn't a figment of his imagination he was seeing. It wasn't in a daze that he saw the once-a-speck object, growing in size as it got closer to him.

At first he thought it was the white light you were supposed to head to when you are dying. He began to let his fingers slip. It was coming closer and closer. *Let it go, let it go.* His mantra of chanting had changed. He took one more brave look on the world he loved that was now bringing him to his end and let his aching fingers lift one at a time. And suddenly he realized. It was a light, but not the light leading to nirvana that he thought it was.

Letting go, he joined the flow of the current. His body moved as an arrow through the water, darting in a single direction and speed. Fast. Fatally fast. He tumbled and rolled through the maelstrom and haphazardly knocked into something very solid. He looked left and again regained vision of the white light. Finally he realized what the mysterious light was. It was not heaven's gate. It was the headlamps of a WakeTec. Not his. Not his ten year old self's prized red and yellow WakeTec. This one must have broken free from the docking station.

Moving parallel, Caspian and the WakeTec traveled. Through quick experimentation, Caspian figured out that if he remained rigid and still, he could control his lateral movement by using his hands as rudders. This way he could direct himself closer to the WakeTec.

Three failed approaches to mount the vehicle ended in a fourth triumphant attempt. Now clinging determinedly to the handle bars, his legs and feet thrashed behind him. With one calculated move, he swung his legs and feet forward and slid into a seated position.

Miraculously, the key was still in place and Caspian wasted no time turning it and gunning the gas. He shot forward like a rocket, hurtling past the weeds and sea life at a blinding speed. He turned the handle bars ever so slightly to the right, testing the strength of the current and the give it would allow him in his chariot of salvation.

Slowly he turned, working his way through the curtain of water. Every foot of progress led him to an area of less turbulence. Every foot was a foot closer to safety, a foot away from death, a foot closer to the ARK. To everyone waiting there for his return. To Nina. A foot. A foot. Just a foot at a time.

Chapter 54
Surface

"I was like a chocolate in a box, looking well behaved and perfect in place, all the while harboring a secret center." – Deb Caletti

The Bay City Fishing Company rig sat 250 feet off the shore. The men and women on board were enjoying their box lunches after a slow morning. Actually, all week, all month, had been slow. It was almost as if the fish were hiding from their nets.

Glum faces chewed on tuna fish sandwiches while glazed eyes scanned the horizon. Minutes of chewing and dazing passed. A disturbance on the water off the starboard side of the boat caused Roy, the rig skipper to stand, adjust his navy brimmed hat and focus his line of vision.

"What is it captain?" a crew member asked.

"Quick! Advance toward the starboard side, now! The fish are teeming! The water looks like its boiling," flecks of spittle and tuna flew from Roy's mouth as he sputtered his instructions. He was so excited. Soon the boat, its captain, and its crew were in the midst of the rippling waters. "Drop the nets! Drop 'em!" the captain hollered.

Thick vinyl corded nets, weighed by standard issued sinkers, plunged into the chaotic water, wanting and waiting to be filled. They didn't have to wait long.

Fish, dolphins, sea creatures of all kinds rammed head first into the nets. Their force nearly knocked the boat over. Instead it dragged the boat for nearly a half mile before it came to a stop.

The chaos on board of the Bay City Company rig suddenly stopped. Stunned silence permeated the deck. And then it erupted in cheers. The load nearly broke the steel rigging lines as they strained to raise the nets. As their catch spilled from their nets their cheers were silenced. For not only did they haul up their intended catch, but dolphins, king mackerels and swordfish littered the deck.

Chapter 55
ARK

"If you aren't going all the way… why go at all?" – Joe Namath

He fought. He fought the current. He fought the current and won.

Caspian was gliding through the water, calmer now than it had been, and the ARK was coming into view. His heart gave a lurch when he saw the damage that had taken place. Extension features, such as sensory poles, cameras, awnings, feeding stations and outside walkways had been ripped from the exterior of the ARK by the whirlpool. Thankfully, the ARK itself looked to remain intact, hopefully the same was true for the people inside.

His heart gave another lurch, no, that was not his heart, it was the WakeTec. Short bursts of speed followed by abrupt stops. Speed. Stop. Speed. Stop. The front display screen was a visual scream of alarms and warnings. The poor vehicle had sustained too many debilitating conditions and it could not go much further. Caspian pointed the vehicle toward what he knew to be a loading dock, although the evidence of it had been washed away. He got within feet of the door before the WakeTec truly expired and he dove headfirst for the door.

Looking over his shoulder he pounded viciously on the door. Attracting the attention of the animals as well as those inside the ARK, a group of three stunned looking dolphins began to swim towards him, swerving stupidly after their merry-go-round morning. While some had been sucked into the magnitude of the whirlpool and been lost, others had found their way back to the ARK. Now they were finding their way to Caspian.

More pounding, afraid to look back. More pounding and then a door open, a swift pull and he was in. Safe. In and safe.

Breathing heavily he slumped to the floor, held in Nina's arms. He looked up, knowing what the others would ask. He was alone.

"Mission accomplished," he managed to say between gasping breaths. "Carl... Carl is, I don't know where he is. He made it into the SQUID. I was ripped away by the current. Carl, 'Cuda, the snakes, I don't know where anyone is. I'm so sorry."

"You're here," Nina whispered into his ear. "We know that much for sure."

Chapter 56
Surface

"The person who says it cannot be done, should not interrupt the person doing it." – Chinese Proverb

Flynn seriously debated about the way in which to get their only adult participant into the Tube and down to the ARK. The hopeful part of her brain wanted to go to the University, and appeal to his compassion and flatter his egotistical intelligence (plainly put: beg). She would beg him to help her. She would tell him everything and then ask him to come with her to the ARK. That was the hopeful part of her brain.

The determined and desperate part of her knew that a rather large chance lay in that plan not working. He might refuse. Even if he did commit to helping, there was also the probability that the University policy and politics would delay the immediate action needed.

So that was it. Flynn decided that she would have to kidnap him. She would also undergo the covert mission of retrieving the displayed documents on the ARK (including blueprints and operational specifics) from the University library. They were located in a special science wing dedicated to the advancement of education in a plethora of scientific fields.

Flynn knew it was there because the wing and ARK display had been dedicated and unveiled a week before the initial departure down to the ARK. All scientists participating in the underwater community living experiment and their families were special guests at the ceremony upon invitation of the University Chancellor.

She had felt more like a science experiment than a

scientist's kid that day. Patted on the head, prodded by questions like, "Are you excited little girl?" from gray bearded men and ladies in navy skirts and blazers. Nevertheless, the terrible experience provided her with the knowledge she needed now, and for that she was thankful.

The kidnapping plan, or adultnapping it might be called in this situation, was almost sickeningly easy to pull off. During lunch one day last week, Flynn called a specific University secretary. She pretended to be Clarissa Turnner, a lead scientist at the Surface Station requesting a visit from the Professor. She, along with the other Surface Station staff would like to update him on a recent development with the pollution eating solution. (This was a safe cover because probably no one at the Surface Station was even aware of the PE-328 release. It was also safe, because it would create enough excitement in the professor to clear his schedule to make the visit possible).

The secretary who was none the wiser to Flynn's impersonated grown up voice, checked immediately with the Professor and confirmed his invitation to the visit within mere minutes.

Flynn then told her specific instructions for the Professor's arrival on the day of the meeting.

"No one is to know he is coming, and neither you nor he can tell anyone the reason for his visit. You see, the press will be invited to the Surface Station shortly after the Professor's visit, and we will announce the progress to the community. Mrs. Worthington, I would really appreciate your integrity and discrepancy with this appointment and information. It would be so disappointing if the information should, pardon the pun, leak."

"I absolutely understand Ms. Turnner. You can rest assured my lips are sealed. Water tight, forgive the returned favor of a pun. I couldn't help myself," the old lady chuckled.

"Quite fine. Quite fine. We look forward to seeing the

Professor at 11:00am in the back entrance area. Remember, have him remain in his vehicle until Surface Station security can escort him into the building."

"Will do."

"Excellent. Have a wonderful weekend," Flynn finished and flipped Nora's phone shut and handed it back to her.

"She bought it?" asked Nora incredulously.

"Totally. Hook, line and sinker. I mean, what sixteen year old do you know that uses the words: discrepancy, appointment, quite and a pun in everyday conversation? I mean, one not preparing for college prep tests and the SAT. She totally bought it. No questions asked."

"Sweet. Now the only thing is how do we get him from the car, past the scientists and into the Tube?" questioned Nora.

"I'm still working on that part of the project yet," Flynn said while munching on a handful of chips. "But no worries Nora. No worries."

Chapter 57
ARK

"The world breaks every one and afterward, many are strong at the broken places. But those that will not break it kills. It kills the very good and the very gentle and the very brave impartially. If you are not one of these you can be sure it will kill you too but there will be no special hurry." – A Farwell to Arms, Ernest Hemingway

Despite the series of tumultuous events early in the day, the sea snakes stood true to their word, and arrived at the south entrance to the ARK a few hours after Caspian's arrival. Leading the way was 'Cuda.

"Man, that is one resilient species!" commented Luke.

"Very true," agreed Caspian, beaming, thrilled that his fishy friend had managed to stay safe. And he was also proud that 'Cuda had managed to convince the sea snakes to come, even after things had ended so unexpectedly at their meeting this morning.

"Greetingsss, human sssea dwellersss. We have come, as we promisssed," Pelamis spoke to Caspian and the others.

"We are ever so pleased and grateful," Professor Bebee said as she stepped forward, and then jumping right to action continued, "Here is how we plan to proceed…"

Pelamis listened intently, nodding his small head, flicking his tongue occasionally – attempting to assess the level of danger. Once Professor Bebee was done explaining, Pelamis turned and briefly communicated in his native language with his nest. It registered to Professor Bebee that if the animals kept their ability to communicate normally, and retained human speaking skills, they essentially the animals were bi-lingual, which put the humans at a distinct disadvantage. Before she has too much time to dwell on her new revelation, Pelamis turned and said, "We are ready."

As planned, Stillman and Sonora donned SCUBA gear and exited the ARK, carrying with them plastic bags. They quickly filled the bags with water and then began carefully loading several sea snakes into each bag. The claustrophobic conditions were not uncomfortable for the snakes, even though once Sonora and Stillman finished loading the nest, the bags looked like giant balls of writhing multi-headed beings, instead of twenty or so individual snakes.

"Aren't you nervous about the bags breaking open?" Nina asked quietly.

"Are you familiar with Ziploc bags?" asked Professor Bebee, who was overseeing the progress of the loading events from her safe vantage point behind the glass.

"Yes, of course," replied Nina.

"Well, just imagine a scientific brand of Ziplocs, with zips at least thirty times stronger." And after a pause and an appraising look at Nina she asked, "Feel better?"

"A little," Nina lied.

They transported the fully loaded bags carefully through the ARK, cautious not to puncture the sides of the bags. Minutes later they were all standing near the doors of the Tube.

Luke opened a filter panel of the Tube to reveal a pool of water that fed, when pressurized, directly into the Tube. Pelamis managed to wiggle his way to the side of the bag and nodded. The bags were carefully lowered into the hole and prodded further into the Tube. Then, on a silent command, the plan burst forth into action.

Pelamis and his nest bit the envelope of the plastic bag with their razor sharp fangs, shredding it to pieces, and swam full speed up the Tube. The puffer fish never saw them coming. Shocked, they fired the only defense they had and expanded to full form. They tried fruitlessly to swim away from their natural predator, but failed. The snakes attacked, succeeded and feasted.

The crew of the ARK watched helplessly from a Tube camera, usually used to track comings and goings of supplies and people to and from the ARK. The urge to cheer on their current hope of survival beat out their guilt and despair of killing so many fish. High fives were passed around as hoots and whistles filled the air. Then, it became suddenly silent.

"What do we do next?" asked Nina.

"Next," explained Professor Bebee, "we wait."

Chapter 58
Surface

"You may be disappointed if you fail, but are doomed if you don't try." – Beverly Sills

Alex had managed to keep his promise, despite the break up, and volunteered to help the girls in their project. He saw his opportunity to create mass chaos and distraction dangling from a crane, its arm and loot extended high above the rest of the incoming packages. He knew that he would have to time it perfectly. For the first time in his life he wished to be his younger brother, who had spent countless hours at the Bay City Skate Park, much to the chagrin of his father. Having a skater son with long unruly hair and an attitude to match was not what political figures dreamed of showcasing in their very public lives.

But his brother he was not, and this he must do. So he took a deep breath, re-grasped the black rubber handles of the bike and pushed off the edge of the unloading ramp.

Since he had been hiding in the very back of the delivery truck, not one of the scientists saw his quick descent down the steep ramp. Three quick pumps of the pedals to another ramp, and then up, up soaring through the air.

Miraculously, he had good aim and gracefully passed the suspended net of fish. As he did so, Alex pulled the bottom release cord on the fish net and sent the fish falling, splattering on the scientists below.

He was so engrossed in the success of his bike jump and the release of the fish, Alex forgot to be concerned about the second half of the daredevil jump. The landing.

He crashed into the pavement first, then a curb and then mercifully into the grass. The commotion of the surprising entrance of the fish to the receiving dock scene was such that the hero of the moment was allowed to limp away and pray that the rest of the project was going as well. Okay, as well, but with maybe a few less bruises.

Chapter 59
ARK

"Until the day when God will deign to reveal the future to man, all human wisdom is contained in these two words, - wait and hope."
The Count of Monte Cristo, Alexandre Dumas

Flynn will be here soon. Or at least she should be. Please, for Poseidon's sake please let her make it. Caspian thought. He was trying very hard not to let his nervous feelings show, but after the things they had been through, it was difficult to remain calm, in control, and a confident leader.

Yes, a leader. That is what I have become, Caspian thought. *On those stupid college applications when they asked for a time when I have shown leadership, I now know what I will answer. Although that won't make much of a difference if I don't make it out of here alive.* He continued to brood. But he quickly squashed that thought and others as the remaining members of the ARK joined him in the Tube Receiving Station.

"Did you finish your jobs?" Caspian asked the others. Nods and small murmurs of obedience were all he got in reply. This meant that huge thick curtains had been hung and dropped over the large observation wall, blocking any sight to the inside of the ARK. It also meant that all remaining food had been either stored and packed ice in the kitchen or divided up amongst knapsacks, one for each person. Each knapsack also included a fully charged converter, a bottle of water and a few basic first aid supplies. Mobile, and ready to go if necessary. Although, no one had any idea where they would be going if they left the ARK.

Jobs completed, all they had left to do was wait for Flynn's hoped upon arrival. Too tired to even pace. They all sat in front of the closed Tube doors and looked for the early signs of its arrival.

Chapter 60
Surface

"Great thoughts speak only to the thoughtful mind, but great actions speak to all mankind." ~ Emily P. Bissell

Anxiously awaiting his special escort into the Surface Station, the Professor was sitting in the back seat of a black Chrysler with darkly tinted windows. He was daydreaming of the supposed press conference to come, when he would yet again get to be a part of a scientific event to shock the world. He enjoyed the behind the scenes science, but he couldn't deny that he loved the fame that he had earned and that was now almost guaranteed to come with any project in which he was involved.

His daydream had gotten to the point of cameras flashing as he concluded what he was sure to be a monumental speech in environmental science history when his cell phone rang. He had no need to wonder how Ms. Turnner had gotten his private unlisted number, because it was given to top level scientists at the station to contact him in case of emergencies with the ARK.

"Ms. Turnner," he assumed, "hello."

"Good afternoon Professor. I have to apologize for the informality of what I am about to request, but I am just finishing up some notes on a conclusive experiment. Would you mind letting yourself in the back door and meeting me in laboratory B?" mimicked Flynn in her adult voice.

"Not a problem at all," answered the Professor.

"Professor, would you do me one other small favor and send your car away? I'm sure that if anyone saw your vehicle here, they would guess that something big and important is going on," said Flynn, crossing her fingers (and her toes) that the Professor would comply. The last thing she needed was for a staff member of the Surface Station staff to see the Professor's car and come looking for him throughout the station.

"Again, not a problem Ms. Turnner. I must admit, I am so curious and excited to see what you have to show me, that I'd do most anything you asked."

"Well I'm glad to hear that," replied Flynn. "I promise you sir, you couldn't even dream of what we have to show you. Don't waste another minute, come on in. The code for the back door is 86-275." *He said he'd do anything* she repeated to herself and then smiled. Quickly her smile faded as she remembered the small window of time she had for the Tube to remain open. The puffer fish were cleared out now, she had checked that upon her arrival, but just exactly how long they had a clear path down to the ARK no one knew. Hopefully the enemy did not have a backup supply of troops attempting to infiltrate the Tube system.

The Professor got out of the car, and directed the chauffeur through his rolled down window that his services would not be needed until later in the afternoon. Mrs. Worthington would call him when the car was needed again. Then, he walked to the back door, entered the code and let himself in. He walked down the corridor and, only getting lost once, found himself in Lab B.

There, he surprisingly found Nora in a white lab coat. Only, he had no idea who Nora was, so this hardly registered to him as odd.

"Hello," said the Professor, "I'm looking for Ms. Turnner. Have you seen her?"

"Yes. She just left to drop something off in the Tube. They are sending a shipment down tomorrow for the new... well, you know..." and then Nora dramatically whispered, "the pollution eating solution. I am not supposed to say anything, but I know you are important enough to know about it, so I
didn't see the hurt in telling you the truth. She asked me to have you meet her there."

"Thank you dear," said the Professor as he nodded his head toward her and backed out of the room toward the Tube. *Flynn was right, flatter this man's ego and he'll do anything. Like a tamed and trained animal in a zoo,* thought Nora.

Nora peeked around the corner and watched the Professor walk away. She tiptoed as quickly as possible down the hallway just in time to see the Professor poke his head into the Tube and then, step all the way in. He was looking just where they wanted him to. Staring, reading, just like they wanted him to. And as he was reading, staring, reading, staring, trying to comprehend what he was looking at, Flynn gave Nora one last big hug and then crept into the Tube.

At that moment, the moment that Flynn was completely inside the Tube, Nora pushed the button. The big red, start of the disembarking, pressurizing the cabin for descent, going down to the ARK button.

From the inside of the Tube, the first minutes of the trip are unnoticeably silent. In fact, if you didn't know the button had been pushed, you would not know that your journey to the bottom of the ocean had begun. The Professor was in this situation and did not know that such a journey for him had started. But like it or not, started it had.

Flynn waited another minute before standing up and walking toward the Professor and the material that was so engrossing him.

"Flynn hello dear, I wasn't aware that you were working at the Surface Station while on your little trip to the surface." he said with the cheerful tone of a grandfather. *Apparently he is still unaware of his immediate fate thought Flynn. Good, the more seconds pass, the more unlikely it will be that anyone can reverse the descention process.*

"I'm not working here Professor." Flynn answered honestly.

"Oh, just come for a visit then?"

"No, not exactly Professor."

It was at this precise moment that the passengers in the Tube became audibly aware of their travels downward. The Professor recognized the sound immediately and spun on his heel to face the closed stainless steel doors of the Tube. Shock was the first emotion to reach his face, panic was the second and rage was the third.

Flynn was prepared to face these feelings and sat quietly down in a passenger chair and watched as the grown man pounded relentlessly against the steel barriers blocking him from exiting the Tube.

Suddenly he turned to face her.

"I demand an explanation young lady. Just exactly what is going on here?" he spoke in his firm, dictatorship voice that figures of authority perfect over time.

"I have no problem telling you Professor, but it is an extremely long tale, and as you know, the ride takes 63 minutes to the ARK so you may want to sit down," said Flynn in a calm, even voice.

Of course the Professor refused and for the first nine minutes paced and fumed across the small expanse of the Tube. Flynn internally laughed, remember herself at a time that seemed lifetimes before, pacing in such a manner of impatience.

Finally the Professor gave into taking a seat, but even then he did not look at Flynn, but instead stared at the floor and picked nervously at thread on this coat cuff. After a short time he had more than a short thread in this hand, having unraveled a centimeter or more of fabric from his Italian suit sleeve. It was then that he looked at Flynn expectantly, as if saying, I'm not going to ask again for the reason for this escapade, so you better start telling me. NOW.

"Well," started Flynn, "since we only have an estimated 49 minutes left on our journey before arrival, I will make this as short, yet informative, as I can."

To his credit, the Professor was a very good listener as Flynn told the story. She told him about the giant glitch with the PE-328 release, the missing adults, their planning, the fight against the creatures and where the children and remaining scientist stood now in their disheveled form of the once magnificent ARK. When she had finished talking they both sat silently for nearly a full minute. Flynn silently wondered if she had induced a small stroke within the Professor's brain, or a mild heart attack at the very least. She was about to check the breathing and pulse of the figure sitting beside her when he finally spoke.

"So, you figured if anyone could help, it would be me," the professor reasoned.

"Yes, well you and me. I have a greater understanding of the computer network in the ARK. You see, no offense, I am not particularly fond of the water, and so whenever doing experiments and out-of-ARK missions, I always volunteered to run the control station. No one else minded because they would rather be out and about, exploring and what not. I guess it resulted in a somewhat skewed understanding of the technical process and equipment in the ARK. So, yes, I am counting on you and I to be the heroes who rush in and save the day."

"Well, you have high standards, I cannot deny you that," the Professor said and Flynn nodded. Now it was her turn to look at the floor. When she said it out loud and had a genius like the Professor listen to her now seemingly childish plan, she wondered what she had gotten them both into. Gotten them all into, because this plan was all they had to save her family, friends, and the ARK.

"Well, I can see from your packed supplies that you have thought this plan well through young lady. So in the remaining 21 minutes we have on this trip, why don't you fill me in on what we are going to do to make this fairy tale have a happy ending?"

Renewed by his faith in her, Flynn sparked to life to tell him her plan and what his role would be. They sifted through the supplies, materials, maps and blueprints to work out what would need to be a heroic, faultless, and bold effort. An effort that those who waited to greet them desperately needed.

Chapter 61
ARK

"Just when you think all is lost, the future still remains."
– Robert Goddard

    As the Tube doors slid open, the three Brinestone siblings' faces met for the first time in over three months. Eyes locked, they could see no farther than each other's faces. But Flynn did not need to look around to know the true devastation that had come upon the ARK. It was all plainly written on her brothers' faces. In an instant she knew she had done the right thing.
    Hundreds of unsaid thoughts passed between Caspian and Flynn in her first moments back in the ARK. Most of them would stay unsaid, some eventually would come out. But for now, an understanding passed between them, however tense it may be.
    As Flynn moved forward out of the Tube, her body and large traveling pack revealed the figure of a distinguished looking man. "I thought we could use some back up." She started in way of explanation, and continued when met with blank stares, "Everyone, this is Solomon Sorenson. And he has come to help. And so have I, because after all, this is our home."

Author's Note

"There is no better feeling than when you write something you know is a piece of you and that, at some point, is going to communicate with someone else." - Alanis Morissette

This book is very much a part of me. In the seven years it took me to write, edit, rewrite, share, write and edit again, I have transformed into a writer, a being completely different from when I started. The quotes that start each chapter are a collection of words that flesh out my teen and twenty something years. They come from poets and musicians, celebrities and confidants, motivators of spirit and encouragers of craft. Thank you a hundred times over to these masters of the written word. In the same manner, thank you also to the amazing authors who continue to entertain and inspire me, specifically: Maggie Stiefvater, Jennifer Donnelly, Ken Follett, George R.R. Martin and Kate DiCamillo. Even if we never meet, I consider you friends.

I want to also offer a heartfelt appreciation to my family, those under my roof, down the road and far away - for their continued support in this project. Matt, thank you for the time you carve out of our crazy kid-filled days for me to do what I love. Thank you, Mom and Dad, for your editing eyes, listening ears, kind words and encouraging support.

Thank you to my team of readers, editors, and idea sounding boards, specifically: Beth, Sarah, Becky, Andrew, Lynn and Emma. You helped me present the best product possible. I am grateful for your honest critiques and feedback, and also for your colored pens!

Finally, thank you to the readers who joined me on this journey. I hope I haven't led you astray and that you have faith enough in me to pick up this book's sequel and the many other adventures that follow.

Happy Reading!
Amanda Zieba

About the Author

Amanda Zieba is a published fiction and nonfiction writer by night and teacher, mother, and wife by day. This is her first young adult novel. She lives in Wisconsin with her husband and two sons. When she is not reading or writing, she enjoys scrapbooking, exercising and traveling to see family.

Previous Books by Amanda Zieba
Orphan Train Riders: Charles' Christmas Gift
Orphan Train Riders: Joanna's Journey
Orphan Train Riders: Irish Strong William

Nonfiction Work by Amanda Zieba can be seen at:
http://contributor.yahoo.com/user/1533842/amanda_zieba.html

Made in the USA
Charleston, SC
22 January 2014